JACK TAKES A WALK

A Jack of All Trades novel

DH Smith

Earlham Books

Published 2024 by Earlham Books
Book design & cover art by Lia at Free Your Words

ISBN: 978-1-909804-65-4

PART ONE:
CAST & SETTING

Characters

Jack Bell...*Builder/sleuth*

Mia Bell...*His daughter/sleuth*

Alison Bell....................................*Mia's mother, Jack's ex-wife*

(DC) Nova Taylor........*Jack's maybe-girlfriend, a Detective Constable*

(DI) Fayyad Kamani.........................*Nova's boss, a Detective Inspector*

Penny Hicks....................................*A maths professor, a walker*

Mike Rayner......................*Hedge fund manager, walk leader*

Fiona Jones......................................*Housing worker, a walker*

Deneb Ali...*Physicist, a walker*

Phil Butt...*Artist, a walker*

Liz Greene.............................*Retired social worker, a walker*

George Taplow.......................................*Penny's ex-husband*

Mrs Elks.....................................*Shop owner, Jack's employer*

Chapter 1

Jack needn't have rushed. Penny wasn't here. He had taken a cubicle and told the waiter that he was waiting for someone. At least, he hoped he was. Jack had cancelled this date several times while vacillating over his relationship with Nova. On, off, on, off. Off. A month cooling off, she had called it. He hadn't wanted to cool off as it felt like that would be the end. Once split apart, they wouldn't get back together again. Not that it was an easy relationship. Nova, fed up with his complaints when she had to cancel. He, fed up with her last-minute cop-outs. It ruined their time together.

'I'm a detective,' she had said. 'My time is not my own.'

Take it or leave it, were the words implied. And the cooling off, which both of them sensed wasn't that at all. Somewhat brutal. But that's the way relationships went. They either worked or not, and at least one party got bruised in the break.

Four weeks ago. And no word from Nova. Not that he had contacted her either. So here he was, free, in Pizza Hut waiting on a date. Someone new, non cop.

If she turned up.

Jack glanced at his watch, ten minutes late. Would this begin and end like Nova? All those cancellations, a texted apology, with him waiting outside the cinema, in the restaurant, or waiting on the Flats with his telescope.

This was a poor start. He looked at his watch again. Eleven minutes late. Should he phone her? But his phone was on. He was here. It was down to her to make her apologies. Or to stand him up.

1

Jack had been unsure what to wear. A suit? But that made the date feel like he was going to a wedding or a funeral. Besides, he hated suits. Felt imprisoned in a banker's uniform. So he had settled for casual. Jeans, a long sleeved green top, and trainers. He'd shaved and showered, so was presentable, casual. Be at ease was the mantra, but he was not at ease. How could you be, when meeting a stranger who you have told, without telling, that you are lonely. Of course, the same could be said about her. With the possible savage postscript, as either could say, as they parted, nice meeting you but no thanks.

A ruthless transaction. Some things stated, some things not. All prejudices in play. Looks and words, how she eats, what she eats, her clothes, her hair. Silences, how words meet or grate. So unlikely to be right, to work out, to hit it off. Suppose one in ten were a fit, he mused, though it could be one in twenty, but suppose one in ten, then there was a ninety per cent chance this was a waste of time. A write off, both thinking how much longer must I endure this, as they ate pizza and tried to keep smiling.

So why was he even bothering?

But a 10% chance of a strike, was not no chance. Then again, she might be his 10% but he not hers. He'd suggest a second date, and she'd politely decline. Or perhaps she'd put him on the spot and say, shall we meet again, and he'd want to decline. Or maybe, this almost made him laugh, he'd invite her out for a night with his telescope. Not here, on neutral turf, but on his home ground, over the Flats on a frosty evening.

That would have to be after the 7th date. When she was prepared to put up with mud and cold.

Such hard work. Worse than a job interview. Being judged, looked up and down, marked, ticked for this and that.

Except she hadn't shown up. Five more minutes, then he'd leave.

Jack looked around the cafe. Fairly busy, a smell of hot tomatoes, cheese and spices. Green leatherette seating, two chefs in the kitchen area furiously making up pizzas from standard bases, adding the bits and pieces on hand for the topping, and sliding them into the grill. Two waitresses in standard uniform with notepads. One young, not much older than his daughter. Could be a student, the other more matronly. The cubicles on either side of him were full. One with a family, the other with a couple. On the noisy side.

He watched the door, at one end of the floor to ceiling window onto the Broadway. Fifteen minutes. He'd best order something, or wait outside. He didn't feel like a pizza, not sitting here, resentful on his own.

'Excuse me.'

He looked up at a woman whose face was familiar. Her photo! Of course!

'Are you Jack?'

She was short, a few inches over five feet. Curly brown hair, efficiently cut, a little make up, purple lipstick. A matching purple jacket with no lapels, over a pink blouse with a frilly collar, a light brown handbag with a long strap over her shoulder, purple nails. It was the colour of the day.

'I am,' he said. 'You must be Penny.'

'Thank heavens.'

She sat down opposite. And in the seconds of her sitting and removing her jacket, he automatically sized up her figure, face, hair, the instant once-over. Not bad, maybe better than not bad. She smiled, so maybe he wasn't bad.

'Have you been here all along?' he said, as she certainly hadn't just come in. He'd been watching the door.

'Sitting over there for the last quarter of an hour.' She pointed over the heads of the chatter and busyness.

He smiled, in relief. 'Didn't see you. I was almost giving up.'

'Ditto.'

It was a smile contest, suffused with hope. Though tension remained. The first few minutes were always so important. She had a confidence about her, the way she had sat down and taken her jacket off. Taking ownership.

'Come far?' he said.

She shrugged. 'Walking distance.'

'Me too.'

'Compatible so far then.' She grinned, perfect teeth.

'That's a low bar,' he said.

'Shall we put it up an inch?'

'High jumps always end in failure,' he said.

'Like most relationships.'

He was unsure what to make of that. That she was fussy, had been through quite a few relationships.

'One can but try,' he said.

'Of course.' Her smile was disarming. 'Why else would I have come?'

The young waitress came over, pen poised.

'Would you like to order, sir, madam?'

'I'm not that hungry,' Penny said over the table. 'Perhaps we could share a pizza. Except I'm veggie.'

'Fine by me.' He took a deep breath. 'And I don't drink.' Relieved to get that out of the way before complications set in.

'No onions for me,' she said, screwing up her face in distaste.

'No olives.'

Both laughed as their idiosyncrasies became public.

'Give and take,' she said. He nodded, just as she added, 'You give, I take.'

He looked at her quizzically.

'A joke! A joke,' she exclaimed. 'In poor taste, especially after three minutes' acquaintance.'

Her face was very animated. She was a risk taker, he reckoned. She was looking at his face too, and seeing what?

'Shall I come back in a few minutes?' said the waitress.

'Please do,' said Penny.

The waitress went away, and was beckoned to a nearby table.

'Wonder what she's thinking,' said Jack.

'I don't think she cares.'

He could smell Penny's perfume, intermingled with hot tomatoes and mozzarella.

An awkward pause. She was looking around the cafe.

'Do you realise nearly all the tables have prime numbers at them, except us?'

He hadn't realised. Hadn't thought about it.

'Two is a prime number,' he said, his daughter had told him so. 'So we are prime. There's a couple of ones here too.'

'It is arguable whether two is prime,' she said.

'Why?'

She smiled. 'It's prime because it's divisible only by itself and one. That's the rule for prime numbers. But it's not prime because it's an even number. So take your choice, but show your working.'

'Are you a maths teacher?'

She smiled. 'I'm a maths professor at Queen Mary University, Mile End.'

That pushed him back. Out of his class? Utterly educated, with more degrees than a thermometer. Then again, she was here. Clever as she was, lonely as he was.

'What's the highest prime number?' he said.

'There isn't a highest.' Then put a finger in the air as if to a class. 'I qualify. We haven't found it, and we've got into trillions of trillions. But the computers crack on.'

'I like big numbers,' he said. 'My daughter and me, she's seventeen, we worked out the number of kilometres in a light year...'

'Lots.'

'Around nine and a half trillion. And the Andromeda Galaxy is two thousand light years away, and that's a near neighbour...'

She laughed. 'This is a most peculiar conversation.'

'Sorry.' He'd already strayed into astronomy, gabbling away. Nerves.

'Don't be sorry. I've been on half a dozen of these dates, and mostly been quite bored.'

'So why do you carry on?'

5

'I've wondered that myself.'

'Maybe you are too clever. All your degrees make the rest of us dumb.'

'You're not dumb, Jack.'

He laughed. 'You should talk to my ex-wife. She will fill you in on my dumbness.'

She blew a raspberry. 'I've had two husbands and wouldn't give either as a reference.'

'Yet you keep trying.'

'I am looking for the largest prime number.'

'You have just said there isn't one!'

'What I added, if you recall, was that we haven't found it yet.' She laughed heartily.

The waitress returned.

'Are you ready to order now?' Pencil and pad at the ready.

'Number 11,' he said. 'That's prime and veggie.'

'And delicious,' said the waitress.

'And two plates,' said Penny. 'And water.'

The waitress left.

'What do you do, Jack?'

'I'm a builder.' He shrugged. 'Small jobs, I work mostly on my own.' He hesitated, should he go on, his latest foray. Then thought, what did it matter? 'I've decided to branch out. Well, change completely.'

'Do tell.'

He was watching her closely. Was she just being polite or actually listening? Should he really tell a stranger his next step, which could be a career change or arrant stupidity. She took a sip of water, she appeared to be waiting. So far, only he and his daughter Mia knew.

'You were going to tell me about your change of direction. Though don't, if it's too early. Some things have to be kept under wraps at the start, I appreciate. They could come to nothing, so...'

'I'll tell you,' he interrupted. 'I'm working in a shop on Woodgrange Road in Forest Gate. Well, it's not a shop yet. I am fitting it out as a curtain shop. But I am doing it on the cheap in exchange for a year's rent on the back room.'

'For a builder's office?'

Their pizza came. The waitress placed it on the table with cutlery, a cutter and two plates. It had tomatoes, red peppers, lots of cheese, and mushrooms. The waitress left them. Penny took up the cutter and sliced it in two. She lifted the platter and pushed half the pizza onto each plate.

'Take your pick,' she said. 'Do go on.'

The waitress returned with a jug of water and two glasses.

'Enjoy,' she said, as she left them.

Jack waiting until she was far enough away, then leaned forward to tell his secret.

'I am setting up as a private detective.'

She didn't laugh, which was a relief. And asked questions, always a sign of a listener's interest. Such a thing for him to say, though. A boast almost, to actually call oneself a private detective. But he justified himself by telling her that he'd had some success helping the police our with various cases. Though, it was his daughter Mia who had suggested he should have a go himself. There was no competition locally, she'd told him. For a good reason, he'd countered her, where's the demand?

But she had persuaded him to give it a go. Mia offered to help out. And Nova might have been useful – which Jack didn't say, as he'd have to say who Nova was, why she might help in her role as a police detective. And very likely wouldn't, things being as they were between them.

'Have you begun yet?' said Penny. 'Your detective work.'

They were eating the pizza. It wasn't bad. He was eating too quickly. Half a pizza wasn't really enough. But it would have to be. She ate more slowly, more delicately, whereas he was used to short lunches at work, and so guzzled quickly.

'My daughter has set up a website: Forest Gate Investigations.'

He looked at her. She still wasn't laughing.

'That's the gateway,' he went on. 'Either no one will come. Or who knows?'

'If you ever need a mathematician,' she said.

'Who knows?' he said.

They were silent a little while, eyes holding eyes across the table. He felt a click of attraction. She was holding his look, not eating, her fork in the air with a piece of pizza. Blue eyes emphasised by blue eyeshadow. Was he a sucker because she was listening? Or was she too held in mutual vibration?

When they finished their pizzas, they had a coffee. Chat came easy once they had opened up, he even told her about his telescope and his nights observing on Wanstead Flats.

'I belong to a walking club,' she said in return. 'East London Walkers. Have you heard of it?' He hadn't. 'Fairly small, maybe eighty members.' Her face brightened. 'There's a walk on Saturday. Forest Gate to Theydon Bois. Do you fancy it?'

Chapter 2

What do you wear for a walk? 13 miles, she'd said. That's a fair stretch. He wasn't sure he was up to it. She had reassured him, just put one foot in front of the other. So boots. All he had was his work boots. They were well worn in. He gave them a polish but they still looked scuffed. Like work boots. The soles were OK with some grip in them, as she'd told him it could be muddy in the forest. Two pairs of socks, OK. He had a half clean, half dirty pair of jeans, but jeans are jeans. Who wears 'em clean but hipsters who then rip them at the knees. A black woolly hat, hoody jacket, and jumper in his backpack, just in case there was a blizzard.

It was when he was halfway up the road, that Jack realised he hadn't any water or food. He thought of going back and making sandwiches, but a glance at his watch told him it was too late for that. He'd buy what was needed on the way. At least he'd eaten this morning, keeping his diabetes at bay. Little and often was the slogan. Beans on toast for breakfast and tea, that should keep him going for a couple of hours. But 13 miles! How long would that take? What state would he be in? He worked hard all week, and here he was, about to work even harder on his day off.

What you do for love!

Or the possibility of it. It was her thing, walking, so he'd have to have a go. And they could chat, maybe get closer, as they wound their way through the forest. Pity there wasn't just the two of them. Then again, maybe OK this way. She was an experienced walker, fitter than him, but there were bound to be some slower ones he could keep up with.

Jack hoped he could make it.

He was nervous at seeing her again, hoping it would go right. A step forward, rather than one back, or into a ditch. The weather was not bad for mid October, not cold yet. No rain was forecast, but if it rained then he'd put up his hood and bear it. He'd worked through rain often enough, never pleasant; cold wet days were the worst.

They'd be heading up to Epping Forest, over Wanstead Flats. A few years back, he'd been involved in burying a body in Epping Forest. One of his more stupid escapades. A woman involved, of course. He being a gent: *of course I'll bury a body for you*. And then having done the dirty deed, he'd lost interest in her.

Typical.

Let's hope today goes better.

The plane trees on Earlham Grove were just losing their leaves, half or more to go. They lay on the ground like stranded jellyfish. So much work sweeping the away each year. Why does the tree have to dump them? His daughter would know the answer to that. In the sixth form, studying biology and Spanish, and getting too clever. Even challenging him on astronomy. He'd have to get a book out of the library to stay ahead.

He passed Forest Gate Community Garden, a woman in there sweeping leaves, the seasonal occupation. Maybe she would know why trees lose their leaves. Though some of them didn't seem to know much more than he did.

Jack glanced at his watch. Five minutes to go, for the meet up at Forest Gate station. Convenient it was nearby. He turned the corner into Woodgrange, the local high street, trembling a little. It had been good in the pizza house. Lots to talk about. She was so brainy. A maths professor! How would she and his daughter Mia get on? Always a consideration with any girlfriend.

If she was going to be that.

Mia wasn't happy when he had started going out with Nova, as she wasn't cop friendly, encountering too many on demos in her eco forays. They were the enemy, protectors of the status quo, right or wrong. He had been piggy in the middle in too many of their rows. But later on, both cooled off and got friendly, keeping off thorny topics.

He passed the Co-op which reminded him of food he didn't have. And there they were, the walking group, outside the red brick station, near that odd lighthouse of a kiosk that changed hands quicker than a relay baton. Seven or eight men and women, all boots, anoraks and backpacks, broken into groups chatting. Their gear making him aware of what he'd slung together.

Too late to go shopping.

And heavens! That was Nova, of all people, she was side on in her green jacket and yellow woolly hat. Talking to a woman about the same size, in a red anorak, her back to him, slim, brown curls coming out of her hat. She half turned as she held out an arm to indicate something. It was Penny, a pale blue silk scarf poking out of her collar.

The two of them here.

In half panic, he thought of turning round and scuttling home. Cowardly, but it would save awkwardness. His feet were undecided and kept walking into the machine gun fire. Then Nova spotted him, pointed him out, and Penny turned and waved.

Jack waved back. 'Hi!'

He walked in, confident as a cat, seemingly. Penny gave him a peck on the cheek. He would've pulled away with Nova there, but what would that say?

'What are you doing here, Jack?' said Nova, hands on her hips, indicating he wasn't welcome.

'I invited him,' said Penny. 'That computer date I was telling you about.'

'Should've guessed. You gave me enough clues. Well, well.'

The two women were the same height, Penny slim, Nova was stocky with a blonde ponytail.

'I thought football was your thing,' said Jack to Nova.

'Too many missed training sessions,' she said. 'And when I pulled out of a couple matches at the last minute, they dropped me from the team.'

Penny looked at Jack then at Nova, her maths brain ticking over.

'Are you two an item?'

'Were,' said Nova. 'Strictly past tense. You know how it is. I'd like a few words in private with him, if you don't mind, Penny.'

Penny screwed up her face as she wondered what was going on.

'Feel free,' she said.

Nova pulled Jack aside, out of Penny's hearing. 'I am not a cop,' she said to him quietly. 'I work for the Council. In accounts. Please.'

'Whatever you say,' he said. He could understand why. Better if people didn't know she was a cop. Made sense. People had grudges.

'Thanks, Jack.'

She patted him on the shoulder, and they joined Penny who looked at him with curiosity and some pique.

He said, 'Nova was making it plain, we have come to the end of the line.' Nova nodded. 'So I've been warned off, no restart on offer today.'

'Or any time,' said Nova.

'I don't want to intrude,' said Penny.

She had red lipstick today, and red fingernails. The colour matching technique. Attractive, red worked. And he had free rein as well as Nova had. This could be a good walk with that out of the way.

'It's no intrusion,' said Nova to Penny. 'He is all yours. I'll write you a reference if you want. Just keep him sober.'

'Might I defend myself,' Jack began to say, bruised at the low blow, he hardly ever got drunk and had only once struck a cop, then recalling that he mustn't talk about cops, and struggled for the right thing to say. And kept silent.

A tall man joined them, about six foot three.

He was muscular, with dark brown short hair, clean shaven, smelling of aftershave. He was kitted in all black gear, hat, jacket, boots, backpack, all looking very new and expensive. He put an arm round Nova and kissed her on the cheek.

'So good to see you, my dear.'

Nova kissed him back. Jack wondered whether this was an act for his and Penny's benefit.

'Mike is our leader,' said Nova, once out of the embrace.

'Jack,' said Jack, putting out a hand, which Mike shook.

'Pleased to meet you, Jack.'

'Me, you,' he said, wondering about the man she'd moved on to. What did he have that Jack didn't? Money, for starters, he could feel that in his gear, the boots, coat and backpack. His watch too, and that phone was pretty swish. The latest iPhone. That would be a thousand quid plus. Mike could take her places that were well out of his range. He wondered what his car was. Some low sports model, or a Mercedes, whatever, bound to be many rungs higher than his beaten up van.

He felt a need to get some space between him and the big man.

'Have I time to get a bit of grub at the Co-op?' he said.

Mike looked at his watch, although he was holding his iPhone. A fancy thing, now that he'd got a proper look; Jack didn't catch the make, doubt if he'd know it anyway, thick and silvery with lots of buttons on the side. Nova was certainly going up in the world. What did he do for a living? City slicker or drug dealer?

'Be quick,' said Mike. 'I'm leaving in five minutes whether you are here or not.' Holding up a hand, fingers splayed out to give a Jack an image of how long he'd got.

'Just in and out,' said Jack, setting off.

'I'll help,' said Penny.

She rapidly caught him as they raced to the Co-op, getting through the door before him. At 10 am on a Saturday morning, the store was busy. Queues at the tills and self service, throngs down the aisles. Music was playing but could barely be heard. There were no baskets left.

'I'll pick one up at the checkout, you get shopping,' said Penny.

Jack rushed about, taking a single banana, a strawberry yogurt, a pack of energy bars, a bag of crisps and a bottle of water. Up an aisle, dodging between shoppers, down the next. He was having trouble holding everything, when Penny appeared with a basket. Jack dropped in the items and they rushed to the tills, dribbling through shoppers.

They had a choice which wasn't much of a choice: the self service machines or the serviced tills, both busy.

'You take the machines, I'll take the tills...'

Jack did as he was bid, noting she could be bossy. How was she with her students?

The Co-op was small for a supermarket, but being in the centre of Forest Gate, the shop got very busy with the service slow. Fine, if you weren't in a rush. All Jack could do, glancing at his watch, was push the basket along with his foot as the queue for the machines inched forward.

There came a yell, some excitement, everyone looked over, Penny was waving frantically as if she'd just won the Olympic five thousand metres. She was at the front of the serviced tills, a definite winner worthy of a gold medal.

Jack abandoned his line and raced across to join her. Behind them a woman complained.

'We've a train to catch,' explained Penny, slapping her phone, a slick lie, simpler than trying to explain they were on a walk and had to be there two minutes ago.

He put the items out, packed them as they were checked. And finally paid by card.

Outside, he said, 'That was a madhouse.'

They jogged up to the station, but the walkers had left.

'He takes no prisoners,' exclaimed Jack, breathless.

'Can't be far ahead,' she said. 'They're heading for the Flats.'

They set off, and, as he suspected, she was fast. He scrambled to keep up with her.

'Have you really finished with Nova?' she said.

'Yes.'

What else could he say? In effect, she had dumped him. But he'd seen at once there was no going back. Get over it. She was with Mike the leader. Nova had truly moved on. It rankled, not simply being rejected but seeing her with her new squeeze.

With himself in the uncomfortable situation, with ex and new, maybe new, both here on the walk.

'I won't be used,' said Penny.

He was a step or two behind as she marched on down the high street. She was halted by the traffic lights at Dames Road.

'I know how it goes,' she went on, impatient for the lights to change. 'Get into another relationship to make the other jealous.'

'That's not what we are doing. It's over.'

Did he want it to be over? Did it matter what he wanted, given where Nova was going.

'I wish I could believe you.' She turned to him, looked him savagely in the eye. 'Don't two-time me, Jack.'

'I had no idea she'd be here today. You know that,' he said in exasperation. The lights changed and she crossed with Jack tailing after. 'Do you want me to go home?'

They were across the lights and heading down the road. She was tight lipped. It might be easier if he cried off. Went home. Met up with Penny some less stressful time. If there was one.

She stopped, he almost bumped into her back. She turned, bit her bottom lip and said, 'Stay. We'll see how today works out.'

Penny turned and was off on her route march.

A trial, he thought. If he were caught cosying up to Nova, then he was out on his ear. Expelled by the prof, and kicked in the groin by the cop.

Half of him wanted to go home, the other half striding behind her.

Chapter 3

Jack and Penny caught the others at the Flats. The west side where funfairs set up, with level grassland, here and there scrubby patches with gorse and small trees, a near-bald patch in the centre after the last funfair. Centre Road split the Flats in two, traffic whizzing from Forest Gate up to Wanstead. It was the east side of the Flats where Jack mostly went; there he set up his telescope on clear nights. This side was almost foreign country.

The walkers had halted, about 50 metres away from the road, and were in a circle, as if Mike were about to deliver a sermon. He and Penny joined the circle, making eight altogether. Nova made space for them. Mike nodded as they shuffled in, and continued talking.

'As I was saying, before Penny and Jack arrived, we will be crossing Wanstead Flats, to Bushwood, and then on to the Green Man roundabout, continuing through the margins of forest not gobbled up by development,' he declared, 'through Highams Park, and on till we get to the forest proper at Chingford, where we will stop for lunch. There's a visitors centre, a tea shop and a hunting lodge. After lunch, we will continue along the trails of the forest, taking a break at High Beach, and continue on to Theydon Bois where we have a choice of pubs.'

He looked around at his crew.

'Thirteen miles in all. I am the leader. No one to get ahead of me. Agreed?' His eyes took in the circle, in case there was a rebel in their midst. 'Good. Now, I want you to introduce yourselves, one at a time. Tell us your name and say some-thing interesting about yourself. Not your job, something else.

I'll begin. I'm Mike and I have kayaked from Land's End to Stranraer.'

He thrust out his chest, obviously proud of his Irish Sea escapade.

'Next.'

A slim, black woman, in her late 30s, said, 'I'm Fiona.' Her black hair was in neat, small plaits, which must have taken ages to do, her purple lips gleaming. She wore a green anorak and striking red slacks. 'I have a cat called Marcus Garvey.'

Jack scratched at his thoughts, for something interesting about himself. Telescope, detective, ex-girlfriend here, what, what? A little time yet before his turn and his one stunning fact.

An elderly bald man said, 'I am Phil.' He had the ruddy, puffed face of a drinker and didn't look like he could manage 13 miles. A little portly, his gear was washed out, almost drained of colour, no match for Fiona's. 'I left home at 14 and became a cook on a Lowestoft trawler.'

Impressive, thought Jack. This was getting competitive.

A short elderly woman said, 'I'm Liz.' She had a stocky strength, looking as if she could walk to the moon. She wore khaki shorts, and had stringy legs poking into highly polished brown boots.

'I have a West Ham season ticket.'

Someone Jack could relate to. He went to the London Stadium from time to time.

'I'm Penny,' said the woman next to him. She held up a finger and smiled at her audience, as if letting them into a deep secret. 'My age is prime, I was born the year after Halley's comet returned.'

Jack knew that one. 1986, the comet came, so she was born 1987, making her how old, he rapidly calculated. Prime number. Had to be 37.

'Jack!' called Mike sharply.

Jack held up a placating hand in apology. He'd been too busy doing sums.

'I'm Jack,' he said, grasping for something interesting, something exciting... 'I have a 150 millimetre parabolic reflector.' He saw the blank looks, and added, 'Astronomical telescope. For stargazing.'

Phew! There were nods, so that was OK.

'I'm Nova.'

He had to admit, his ex looked good in her green jacket, her blonde ponytail poking out of her yellow woolly hat. But all he could was look, don't touch. She was well out of bounds.

'I have a black belt in Judo,' she said.

There was a collective intake of breath. A "don't mess with me" message, that he had got loud and clear beforehand.

'I'm Deneb,' said a middle-aged Asian man, in a red anorak, with a single walking stick.

'In Cygnus, the Summer Triangle,' mumbled Jack.

'Please don't speak out of turn,' snapped Mike. Obviously a stickler for rules. How did Nova cope?

'But he is correct,' said Deneb. 'Well done. I am impressed, Jack. Deneb is a star in the constellation Cygnus, the Swan. My name is from the Arabic meaning tail. If there were more of us, it would be apt for me to be the back-marker, but with so few it isn't necessary.'

Jack could see Mike was growing impatient at this extraneous information.

'One thing of interest,' he snapped. 'About *yourself.*'

Deneb breathed in, obviously hurt.

'I came across the Channel,' he said, 'in a very crowded rubber dinghy.'

Impressive, thought Jack, though Mike looked disapproving. At what? That Deneb had been an asylum seeker, a story there, or that he'd taken star billing in hazard and name.

There was a pause, they had been round the circle, while Mike looked them over, doing a quick count.

'Thank you, everyone,' he said. 'There's eight of us. I don't use a map. That is antediluvian.'

Jack struggled at that. But obviously something bad.

Mike held up his iPhone. 'GPS and full Ordnance Survey is the only way to go.' He looked around for any antediluvian rebels, then continued. 'Let's walk. Please keep up.'

He turned and led them off.

Did he have to be so officious, thought Jack. Even so, that was a good icebreaker. Each of them he had something he could chat to them about. He was the telescope, the black woman had a cat called Marcus something or other, probably important, the stocky woman was a West Ham ticket holder, Phil had been a cook on a trawler, Deneb had crossed the channel in an overcrowded dinghy. Who did that leave? Penny with the mathematics telling everyone how old she was if they knew when Halley's Comet came, or could work it out as her age was a prime number. And Nova who could floor them all.

Jack looked up at the sky, being a skywatcher, alert to clouds, to the blue patches, to the movements in the firmament. He wouldn't be out tonight with his telescope, not after 13 miles, likely he'd be flat out on the sofa, aching legs, watching *Match of the Day*. But it would have been a frustrating night with a scope. Some clear blue, true, but swift cloud would quickly smother whatever planet he was looking at. Just as well it was a night for telly.

The short elderly woman was by him as they crossed the Flats, striding over bumpy mole-hilled turf.

'Liz,' he said in recall. 'A West Ham season ticket holder.'

'For my sins,' she grinned. 'I was a steward at the Upton Park ground. But when we moved to the London Stadium, they didn't want us any more.'

'How do you like the new ground?' He corrected himself. 'Hardly new. 2016, they moved.'

She blew a raspberry. 'Give me Upton Park any day, a proper football ground. The London Stadium was built for the 2012 Olympics. An athletics stadium. There's a track round the football pitch. They cover it up in the football season, but it means you are further away. Less atmosphere.' She shrugged. 'I almost gave up on the Hammers. But they're my team. So I cope.'

'I preferred Upton Park too,' he said.

'You a Hammers fan?'

'For my sins.' He mimicked her. 'We were lucky not to get relegated last season. But we're in the top half of the Premier Division this season...'

'At the moment,' she said with emphasis. 'Supporting West Ham makes you a pessimist.'

He laughed with her, and leaned in closer. 'What do you think of Mike?'

'Bossy,' she said in a low voice, looking about her to make sure she wasn't overheard. 'I've been on a few walks he's led. Always lays down the law, but then I don't have to sleep with him...' She guffawed.

Jack joined in. It would have been an unlikely pairing.

'He's with Nova these days,' he said, hoping to get more info.

She shrugged, pulling aside a bramble. 'Won't last. He's had four girlfriends this year. I can't keep up with them. I said to Fran, how's Mike, and she says, 'We broke up, before one of us got killed.' Liz smirked, obviously a key node on the grapevine. 'She and the others, all give the same reason. He wants total control.'

'No possibility of that with Nova,' he said. 'She'll throw him.' Then aware it was a joke, added, 'Black belt.'

They were walking past a patch of burnt ground, black ash scattered with charcoal pieces of twig.

'I saw you talking to her. Were you together?'

'A few months,' he said, lessening their time together, not sure he should be saying anything, as Liz could well be the town gossip. But so what?

'Still keen on her?' She nudged him, a mischievous smirk. This wasn't one for the telling, so he shrugged.

'Just hang around,' she said. 'She'll learn, and you can have another go.'

He wasn't sure he wanted to know that. Best to know for sure their affair was over and done with. Not to be told to hang around to be rejected once more.

A parade of gulls were on a patch of grass in front of them, white and grey, attacking whatever was in the grass. Scornful of these humans, parting as the line of walkers came through, as if recognising them as weedy nature lovers, with not a pack of chips between them.

Mike had stopped at a patch of burnt out scrub and was waiting for them to come in. When they were all there, he said:

'There were over a dozen fire engines here last summer. In the drought, the Flats burnt up like dried newspaper. There's more burnt out areas across the other side. They will regenerate, but if we get more droughts from climate change, we'll get bigger fires and more of them.'

Liz piped up, very animated. 'The biggest fire on the Flats was in the 2018 drought. There were over 30 fire engines present.'

Mike peered down at her, his fingers tapping his over-priced watch.

'Are you leading this walk, Liz?'

Liz pursed her lips but said nothing.

'If there's no more interruptions,' Mike said, daring anybody. He swung his arms round, indicating the ground around them. 'During the war, there were two prisoner of war camps here, Italian and German. The German one was right here, where we are standing. A lot of them were content to be out of the war. Who'd want to be frost-bitten and shot at on the Eastern Front? The camp made their own entertainment: concerts, plays, with lectures on arts and science. Though there were Nazis among them who kept the Hitler doubters in line.'

'Like Islamic State,' said Deneb. Sounding like he knew, Jack thought. He must have a word with Deneb, the star in the Summer Triangle.

They moved on.

Mike took one of many paths, though it would have been easy enough to simply cut through, the only barrier gorse and bramble patches, the trees had given up. But the full sky, that was the glory of flat land, the cops and the army couldn't steal the dome of it, no camps or stables, no developers trying to grab it.

They stopped at Lake House Road, gathered together where Mike halted them. He went out to the middle of the road like a traffic cop, halting the traffic, and they crossed in a group.

Chapter 4

Nova was by his side. It seemed that was the way it went on walks. You choose who to be with, who to avoid. Come and go. Penny was somewhere behind them, he wasn't sure where. Close enough to hear? But certainly keeping an eye out.

'I wish you hadn't come, Jack.'

'Good to see you, too, Nova.'

'We need space.'

He gestured around him, at football pitches and the sky.

'We have it.'

'You know what I mean.'

He did, of course.

'So why are you talking to me?'

'Telling you. Making it clear to you, that we are no longer...'

She hesitated. He reckoned she didn't want to say 'lovers'.

'Over to you and kayaking Mike,' he said. 'Though I hear he gets around.'

'Mind your own business.'

They walked on in silence, each too aware of the other, their mutual past.

'I was surprised to see you with Penny,' she said.

'Mind your own business.'

'Touché.' She looked about, wondering who was in earshot. 'I should leave you. We are already creating gossip.'

You came to me, he thought. I was quite happy, well not happy, to leave you alone. I know the score without you hitting me on the head with it.

'We can be friends,' she said.

He chuckled. The old cliché. The pushing away, the space making, the limiting, whatever 'friends' are and can be.

She had gone, striding ahead, making space.

A dog walker was approaching, a hairy, brutish animal. Jack was thankful he was in a group, halfway down, so others would face the animal first. The dog bared its teeth, and the owner, a young woman, snapped on a leash and stopped. The dog growled as they came through, aching to get at those fast moving legs.

Penny appeared.

'What did she have to say?'

'We can be friends,' said Jack, knowing who she was on about. Hardly clairvoyance.

Penny laughed. 'How often have I heard that one!'

'Sometimes true.'

'Sometimes a polite lie.'

'It was a surprise to see her today.'

'I know that's true, at least. I invited you, so, unless you have a crystal ball, you weren't to know she'd be here.'

'It's awkward.'

'For the three of us.'

He almost expected her to say, we can be friends. The old, old, brush off.

'What did those boots cost you?' She was looking at his light brown working boots.

'25 quid. They've got steel caps.'

'Who are you thinking of kicking?'

She was smiling, so the heat was off, for a few minutes, anyway.

'You have been married twice?' he said.

'At least, you listen. Yes, two husbands. Not simultaneously, I may add.'

He had figured her age. 37. And two husbands already.

'One was a mathematician,' she said. 'He didn't like it when I became his boss.'

Jack laughed.

'It's one thing at work,' she continued, 'but taking the department home too.' She waved a dismissive hand. 'No, no, no.'

'And the other?'

'You want to know who was before you.' She chuckled. 'No builders as yet.'

As yet, thought Jack. What did that mean?

'Lance is a rock singer,' she said. 'Not that successful, though the band had hits in Sweden and Denmark. On tour there, he had his pick of fans, like a kid in a sweetshop. Hardly knew who to go for first. Some under age.' She flipped a dismissive hand. 'The perks of the game. It's why he loved touring, the opportunities. Though, going bald now, classic ageing rocker, still putting it out.' She shrugged. 'I left him to his screaming chicks.'

Mike had halted, stopping the group. When they were gathered in, he said:

'In the woodland, up ahead, is the Witch's Tree. I shall tell you all about its wanderings and evil aura when we get there.' He grinned, as if holding a wicked secret.

They walked on, into woodland.

Jack and Penny were still together. He wanted to know more about her, beyond mathematics and two husbands. He was about to speak, when Penny put a finger to her lips and indicated behind them. Fiona and Phil were getting heated.

'It's utterly ridiculous,' exclaimed Phil. 'Woke gone mad. I couldn't believe it when I read it. She is so English, the epitome of Englishness.'

'Do you feel threatened?' said Fiona. 'An attack on white male privilege.'

Phil was angry, but Fiona was calm, goading him with quietness.

'That is so ridiculous. This is a conversation. It's the way you lot attack. The woke agenda. I can hardly think of anyone more English, more part of the literary canon.'

Who, who, wondered Jack, was so English, the epitome of whatever. Already dangerous ground. Mind your p's and q's, except Phil wasn't, stepping on them willy-nilly.

'You've been drinking,' said Fiona. 'I've seen you taking sneaky swigs from your flask. In vino veritas, Phil. In your case, in vino racism. A little booze and out it comes. Your true thoughts. You can't hide them, booze opens the box and lets your thoughts fly.'

'But Alice in Wonderland!' he exclaimed. 'I can't believe it. Is nothing sacred? A little girl going down a rabbit hole, blonde in a blue dress with a white apron...'

'That's Walt Disney, not Lewis Carroll. The original Tenniel drawings were in pen and ink, no colour.'

'But she wasn't black! Don't tell me she was. She is as English as an Oxford spire.'

'It's called acting, Phil. The girl playing Alice isn't Alice. Is she? She is acting her. Do you see the difference?'

'It's woke gone mad. Alice of all people. So English, it's woke beyond reason.'

'I have seen Maxine Peake playing *Hamlet*,' said Fiona. 'Helen Mirren playing Prospero, an *As You Like It* with three black characters, a black *Uncle Vanya*. It takes no time at all to accept them. They are players. It's acting. Just a story. So a black girl playing Alice? So what? All that matters is her acting. If she's any good. And if she is, no one but you will care.'

'Everything has got to be woke these days. It has taken over everything, everywhere!'

'So tell me what woke means.'

'You of all people should know what it means.'

'I do, but do you?'

'I know what it means.'

'Tell me then.'

'I know what it means.'

'You shouldn't use words if you don't know what they mean, Phil.'

26

That's laying it down, thought Jack. She takes no prisoners.

'No evading now,' she went on. 'What does woke mean, you have been going on and on about it, tell me.'

'A black Alice is woke. That's what it means. It means wrong! Imposed on us by the right-on politically correct Guardian readers, stripping away everything English. That's what it means.'

'It doesn't.'

'It does. And you are an obstreperous woman. You don't mean half of what you say. You're deliberately argument-ative. No respect for English culture.'

'You can't define woke. Can you define English, please?'

'I am not listening to you any more. Go away, go away, with your wokerati agenda.'

Silence behind them. The tirade had ceased. One of them had dropped back. He suspected it was Phil. Perhaps to have another drink and lick his wounds. And to find someone, anyone, who would regard a black Alice as utterly woke.

Chapter 5

They were on a wide path going through woodland, leaves scattered on the trail, oak, hornbeam and ash the trees of the forest. A thin strip of sky above, blue and white, like Disney's Alice dress.

Penny had dropped away. Jack glanced back, she was with Nova. He doubted they were talking about the weather. What was Nova saying about him? Doing him down? Well, it was his turn now. Jack upped his pace until he was by Mike who was looking at his phone which showed a map.

'Great piece of gear that,' said Jack. Flattery always works.

'Did you know this pings up to three or four satellites circling the earth? The satellites measure the time it takes for the signal to get to them. At the speed of light, man! They have the most accurate of atomic clocks. And with three measurements, pinpoint your position. Did you know that, man?'

Jack did. He'd read an article in his astronomy magazine explaining how GPS worked. Caesium clocks in the satellites, accurate to many millionths of a second. But he'd be humble. He'd clocked Mike.

'I never knew that,' he said. 'Always wondered how they worked.'

'It is mind blowing,' said Mike. 'Doing it for millions of users at the same time. Cars, ships, planes, walkers. And those clocks have got to be so accurate...' He stopped. 'Mind you, this one,' he indicated his watch, 'is accurate to a ten thousandth of a second a month.' He peered at Jack's arm. 'What's that bit of rubbish you are wearing?'

Jack was unsure what bit of rubbish he was referring to. Boots, jeans, beanie...

'Your excuse of a watch.'

'It works,' said Jack. 'Tells the time.'

Mike sighed. 'You guys just don't get it.' As if talking to an idiot, he said, 'A watch is just not a timepiece.'

'It isn't?' said Jack, genuinely puzzled.

'It says who you are. And that piece of tat, says you are a cheapskate.'

Jack almost smiled at the man's snobbery, but said nothing. The watch cost him twenty pounds ten years ago, and was fine. He had no need to be accurate to thousandths of a second, or to impress anyone with his jewellery. So maybe he was a cheapskate, better than a gadget snob, as his daughter might have said.

'Your first walk with us?'

'It is.' Jack indicated behind him. 'Fiona and Phil were getting very heated back there.'

Mike pursed his lips. 'Never take on Fiona. She'll cut you off at the knees.'

'Have you been a victim?'

'She has a thing against hedge fund managers, says they are parasites.' He chuckled, then said quietly, 'such are the thoughts of the bitter.'

'What exactly is a hedge fund?' He might as well admit his ignorance.

'Nothing to do with vegetation, Jack.' Mike laughed at his weak joke. 'Hedge funds make money from money. From derivatives, from selling short, from getting in the market and getting out sharpish.'

'Is any of that useful?'

'What does useful mean? We spread money around, force companies to be more efficient. We are the hard and fast cowboys.'

'You taking steers to Dodge?'

'To Theydon Bois via Epping Forest!' Mike guffawed.

Jack grinned. And now knew the source of the iPhone and posh watch. Hedge funds.

'It makes me a good living, Jack. I don't give a damn about the Fionas of the world and their Guardian reading politics.' He splayed his arms out. 'I mean, who on earth is useful these days? Farmers and doctors maybe, who else? I tell you, we are living in the last days. Climate change is going to doom us all. So make money while you can. However you can. The good will drown with the bad. Now, if you'll excuse me, I have the Witch's Tree to find. And I know we are close by.'

Jack dropped back, leaving Mike to his phone app. Doomed eh? He'd like to set him up with his daughter, Mia. Who would eat who for lunch?

It seemed that it was easy to find people to argue with on a walk. And they'd only been walking for an hour or so. A good job too, as if you put them all in a room together it'd be Lord of the Flies. Last man standing.

But you can drop back, walk ahead, cut any conversation short.

He walked on his own a while, thinking about the utility of hedge funds and climate change, drifting to Nova and 'we can be friends', to Penny and her two husbands, to Fiona and her set-to with Phil. At least someone else was getting it and not him.

The ground was damp, but not as wet as he'd been led to believe. A few puddles with leaves floating in them, easy to step over or walk round.

Penny came striding through. Maybe to berate him with some unflattering flak she'd got from Nova, but no, she passed him with a wave and caught up Mike. She seemed agitated. Jack increased his speed to hear what was being said.

A pair of crows passed overhead, screeching to warn of the walkers below.

'Mike.' Penny had caught him up, and held him by the arm. 'We are going round in circles. We have been past that tree twice, maybe three times.'

'I am looking for the Witch's Tree,' he said, deep into his app on his phone.

'Is it that important?'

He took a deep breath. 'Who is leading this walk, Penny? Me or you?'

'You are. But we are going round in circles.'

'The Witch's Tree is on the agenda. You saw it on the email I sent round. And I mean to find it.' He stopped, and waited for the group to catch up. When they were all together, he said:

'We are going to have a snack break.'

'We've only been going for an hour,' insisted Fiona.

'Snack break.' Mike asserted, tapping his watch. 'Fifteen minutes. I am off to find the Witch's Tree. Back soon.'

And he was away, striding down the track. Jack watched him go, turning off a little way down.

Fiona flapped her arms and looked to the heavens for inspiration.

Jack looked about for somewhere to sit and eat. He was feeling peckish, so a snack break was OK by him. Little and often was the doctor's order. A little way off the trail, in the woods, he spied a tree stump. He made for it before someone else did. Jack sat down carefully. It was damp, with bracket fungus coming out the side, but it was here or on the ground. Some of the others, he noted, put down plastic mats. A note for some other time, should he be invited on more walks.

Where was Penny? Gone off for some other thing, as one did in the woods. Eat. It was a few hours since breakfast. He went through his backpack and came up with the yoghurt he'd bought in his hurried rush round the supermarket. A tasty snack, sugar always worked, no matter what the medicos said. Then realised, he didn't have a spoon. Damn.

The yogurt would go off in a few hours, he'd not get it back home, a wasted purchase.

Looking it over in askance, he had an idea. And he peeled off the thin foil cover. He licked it clean. Waste not, want not. Not true, just too smart. He gazed at the foil lid. Could he make it into a spoon? Jack thought how, for a minute, as if it were a problem on a job. Twist that, bend that. Might work. He tore in through the middle, both sides, leaving about an inch of the circle untorn, and, by folding, made two thirds of the foil into a handle. The other third would be the spoon bowl.

A fascinating problem for a desert island, should he marooned with a thousand yogurts and no spoon. Jack messed around with the foil flap, making a putative bowl, folding it this way and that. The others were seated here and there, tucking into their food; he could hear vague chatting but no words. Phil was coming back from a visit to the woods. He felt a little isolated, not part of the conversation. He couldn't see Penny or Nova. He shrugged, they were somewhere, and he had a spoon to finish.

There was a scuffing in the undergrowth behind him. Jack turned. There was a fox maybe ten yards away, watching him watching it. Red with a hairy muzzle, black eyes fixed on him. Was he in its territory? Well, he wasn't moving. He had a task to complete.

Jack worked on his spoon. The handle was firm enough if he held it carefully. It was the bowl causing him trouble. Of course, a scoop! He bent up the sides reinforcing them with folded over foil. The shovel was the width of his thumb, and managed to find enough foil to build up the back where the scoop joined the handle. Pleased with his handiwork, he turned it to examine on all sides, could he patent it?

He turned behind, the fox had gone. Or maybe was watching, waiting for him to go from another vantage point.

Jack picked up his yogurt. There was an ant floundering on the creamy surface. He delicately pulled it out. The ant stuck to his finger in a yogurt glue, he waved it to dislodge the insect but it was stuck. He felt sentimental, and didn't want to crush it, and so gently scraped it on to the side of the stump. He watched the ant wriggling in yogurt on the damp wood. Eat your way out, mate. Enough animal rescue. He dipped his newly fabricated spoon into the pot. It held and he scooped up a little. Yes! Quite childish really, but he had solved his little problem. No spoon, so make one.

Why wasn't he rich, with all these brilliant ideas!

The ant had escaped the gloop, tiny globules of yogurt on its legs. A clumsy, sticky walk, but it was freed and fully fed.

Penny came to join him.

'Is there room on your stump?'

'Just about.'

He shifted, so she could get on. A cosy seating, just touching.

'I like your spoon,' she said, watching him scoop from the pot.

'I shall patent it,' he said.

He'd lost sight of his ant, probably gone into a crack on the stump. A penny whistle was playing. Who, where? Jack looked about. There was Fiona, with the tiny pipe. He recognised the tune: *When the Saints Go Marching in*. She needed a bit more oomph, more bounce. Probably new at the instrument. Not unpleasant.

Penny, by his side, was eating a sandwich. She said, between mouthfuls, 'You're a builder, Jack.'

'Yep. Got a job for me?'

'No, I just wondered what qualifications you have. As a builder.'

'None. Apart from having done it for five years. I left school with no qualifications.'

'None at all?'

'None. I didn't turn up for the exams. Didn't see the point. I'd only fail, hadn't done any work. In the last year I only came into school so I could get in the football team.

And yes, before you say so, it was stupid of me. I've learnt a lot in the meantime.' He took a mouthful of yogurt. 'People think I'm thick as tar because I don't have a bit of paper.' He shrugged. 'School is not the only place to learn.'

Was he trying too hard?

She screwed up her face, maybe annoyed at his downplaying bits of paper.

'I am surprised you can be a builder in this country without qualifications,' she said.

Jack shrugged. 'You just call yourself a builder, and bingo! you are one.'

'No wonder there are so many cowboys.'

Jack laughed. 'I've cleaned up some of their botched work.'

'There should be some official body. Like for doctors and lawyers.'

'I'm not going to start one.'

There came a cry from the trail. 'Everyone!' It was Nova in the middle of the path, arms wide, turning about so they could all see her, calling them in. 'Come here, please.'

Jack and Penny rose and joined her on the path, wondering what this was about. The others came from where they'd been sitting, seven in all.

Nova addressed them. 'I can't contact Mike.'

'He has his phone with him,' said Fiona.

'I've rung him three times,' said Nova. 'It just rings and puts me on to his voicemail.'

'What can that mean?' said Liz.

Nova enumerated on her fingers. 'He's either lost his phone, he's deliberately not answering or he's hurt, so hurt, he is unable to answer.'

Mike is arrogant enough not to answer, thought Jack. A free wheeling outlaw, he'd answer if there's money in it. Big money to satisfy a hedge fund manager. Or sex, of course, but that was not on the menu on this walk.

Then again, who is to say what might be going on in all those tumbling wheels.

'Ring him again,' said Fiona. 'Then we can go down the path, both ways and see if we can hear it ringing.'

Nova rang. She waved them off.

'Go,' she exclaimed. 'Both directions. Come back if you can hear his phone.'

They went down the path, some one way, some the other, looking back at her for direction.

She rang again, and again. Every six rings it went to the annoying voicemail message of Mike saying, '*I can't answer your phone now. Leave your message after the tone.*'

'I can hear it!' yelled Deneb. He waved his arms so everyone could see him. 'From there!' he pointed.

They raced up to where he was.

Nova rang again. The ringing could be heard faintly. They went down the track towards the sound, all concentrating, hands to their ears, hushing each other.

There was a side path. The group took it, the ringing growing louder. And louder as they homed in, crouching like the Indians in Peter Pan following the trail. But they had reached their goal.

They had found Mike.

He was laid out on the path, on his front, face in the damp dirt, arms by his side, the phone ringing close to his right hand.

The group stood round him, fingers to mouths. This could not be what it seemed.

'I'm a police officer,' said Nova, gazing around at them all, full authority in her voice.

'How do we know that?' said Phil.

The others were mumbling their doubts.

'She is a cop,' said Jack.

'And how would you happen to know?' challenged Liz.

'He's her ex,' said Fiona.

Jack was unsure whether this was back up or not, sensing hostility to him from the group, the new guy.

'Back off, everyone. I'm going to look at him,' said Nova. 'And please stay back.'

'You said you worked for the Council,' said Fiona, obviously annoyed at her change of identity.

'I am a cop,' insisted Nova. 'This is no time to argue. Now keep back, all of you.'

Her arms were wide, as she ushered them back ten yards, like pushing sheep out of a field.

They went resentfully. Nova had lied to them, for whatever reason.

Jack backed off with the others, while Nova examined Mike. This must be the Witch's Tree, he thought, with Mike at the foot of it. The tree had thick roots at the front, out of the soil, which were buckled up like the legs of a giant spider. Under them was a sort of cave that a child could crawl through.

Nova was crouched by Mike's head and shoulders. She felt the pulse in his wrist and shook her head. There was a split in the back of his jacket. She put two fingers in and brought them out covered in blood.

There were grimaces all round. Stabbed, thought Jack.

Nova rose, she wiped her bloody fingers on a tissue, an urgency in her voice. 'This is now a crime scene. As a police officer, I am in charge here. Please co-operate, and do not disturb the scene. I am going to phone the police and ambulance. Stay back, Mike is well and truly dead.'

Chapter 6

Nova told Jack to take contact details from the group as they would all need to give a statement to the police. He noted that he was 'told' and not 'asked', but this was no time to have a tiff with his ex, with a dead body close by. He grudgingly accepted authority was needed, someone had to take charge. It was his history with her, his resentment at their change in relationship, at his loss of her.

Jack had a pen in his backpack and found an old invoice which would do to write on. He went round the walkers one at a time, taking names, addresses, phone numbers and emails as Nova had ordered. But it proved fine, the task gave him something to do, instead of being in the group, bewildered, asking questions no one could answer.

At least everyone knew their own name.

Nova moved the group back about 30 yards from the body and the Witch's Tree. They sat by the side of the trail, like abandoned refugees. Phil asked to leave, saying this was a waste of time. He couldn't do anything. No, she said, we all must stay until the police arrive.

It had grown chilly. Or was it the atmosphere? The sky was half blue, half cloudy, oblivious to the concerns of mortals way below.

Jack continued taking details.

Deneb said, when Jack got to him, 'Who could have killed him?'

Not a question he expected to be answered, but Jack said:

'Either one of us, or someone else.'

'Logical,' said Deneb, 'but adding nothing to what I already know.'

'Isn't there a physics thing where a particle can be in two places at once?'

'Yes, in quantum theory,' said Deneb. 'It applies to photons and electrons, but it doesn't apply to murderers.' He smiled weakly. 'Schrodinger's cat may be dead and undead, but not Mike. Nor me, nor you.'

'I was nearly dead once,' said Jack. 'Not that I knew much about it. Half alive, half dead, you might say. Carbon monoxide poisoning.'

'I almost drowned in the channel,' said Deneb. 'There were 35 of us in a boat for 10. They forced us into it at gunpoint. You just hoped the sea would be kind.' He shrugged. 'My therapist says I must talk about it. Not bottle it up, like some secret to be ashamed of.' After a long pause, he went on, 'The boat sank, of course. It was so low on the waves. My wife and son drowned. I was rescued by the RNLI, so they tell me. I recovered consciousness in hospital, I asked about my wife and son and the poor nurse had to give me the bad news. The saddest day of my life.' He shook his head. 'They were very good, the lifeboat people, the hospital, I can't praise them enough, but some days I wish they had left me in he sea.'

'That's awful,' Jack managed to say, imagining how he would cope if told of the death of his daughter.

Deneb wiped his eyes with the back of his hand.

'Excuse me.'

'I am sorry this has to remind you,' said Jack.

Deneb shook his head. 'Everything reminds me. But I am better in the open air. And I can't bottle it up. PTSD, says my therapist. A label for my nightmares.'

Jack wanted to say something comforting, but what could he say? The usual platitudes about time the healer. But what did he know?

All he could say was, 'I am so sorry,' and hold Deneb's arm for a few seconds before moving on to collect details from someone else.

Nova was on her phone loudly giving directions either to the cops or to the ambulance crew. Jack at least had a job to do, but the rest of the group were slumped by the path shell-shocked.

He heard Phil say, 'I knew I should not have come today.'

'How very wise of you,' said Fiona.

'I wouldn't be arguing with you then.'

'Sometimes it's better to say nothing.'

'If you weren't a woman, I'd sock you one.'

'How would that help?'

'It would shut you up.'

Liz intervened, telling them to have some respect, pointing out the corpse. Phil said, it was her fault, starting things. Fiona said, he drinks and mouths off.

A dog walker tried to come through, which took their attention. Nova held him back, saying she was police. He became aggressive and asked for her warrant card. For whatever reason, she didn't have it with her and the dog walker was about to push her aside.

'I wouldn't, mate,' said Jack, coming over. 'She'll throw you up a tree.'

'Her and whose army?'

The dog, large shaggy animal, was snarling, held back only by the man's fingers under its collar. Jack wondered how Nova would handle them both.

'She is a cop,' he said, 'we've found a body.'

Jack pointed Mike out, the dog walker, undeterred, wanted to go and look. And do what? Jack and Nova, arms wide, barred him.

'If you continue,' said Nova, 'I shall arrest you.'

'You are off duty, Miss High and Mighty,' he exclaimed. 'Where's the crime tape?'

'If you continue,' she repeated, 'I shall arrest you.'

It became a staring contest. Why oh why, thought Jack, there's no face to lose here. Except the man's temper had nowhere to go. And Nova was a woman, without a uniform and without a warrant card.

Distant sirens were heard.

'Backup is on the way,' said Nova. 'If you persist, sir, you will be handcuffed and taken to the station and held overnight. Do you want that, sir?'

The dog walker blew out his cheeks. Even through his temper and stubbornness, he could see how this would end. Without a word, he put the lead on the dog collar, thrust up a finger to her, and did an about turn. He walked quickly away with his dog.

'Off to beat up his wife, no doubt,' said Nova, when he was out of earshot.

Chapter 7

The police had arrived. The officer in charge was Detective Inspector Fayyad Kamani, an Asian man in plain clothes, smartly dressed in a bluish grey suit, with a red tie. He was Nova's boss and a school friend of Jack's. Almost a family affair.

Jack was asked to give the contact details he had collected to a uniformed officer. But the man chosen couldn't read Jack's writing.

'I had nothing to rest on,' protested Jack, though his writing wasn't neat at the best of times.

In the end, it was decided that Jack would dictate the information and the cop would write it in his notebook. Time consuming it might be, but Jack had no pressing engagements.

Two uniformed officers put out crime scene tape, pushing the group further back. The blue and white tape was tacked to trees, and a few posts were put in for attachment. With the coming and goings, it had become the classic crime scene.

A police doctor competed with a police photographer over the body. Both had put on CSI coveralls, being identified only by the camera and the medical bag.

'He's dead. You can wait,' said the photographer snapping away.

He took extensive photos of the body from all angles.

'Just a minute or two,' he kept saying. 'We must have photos as we have found him. Then he's all yours.'

A police officer came along, carrying three folded chairs. Jack couldn't see the vehicles, but they must be fairly close.

The interviews of the walkers began. Not full interviews, they would be taken at the station. These were preliminary.

Nova and her boss, DI Kamani, took two of the chairs, Fiona, the first to be interviewed, the other. Jack wondered whether Nova should be an interviewer. All the walkers, surely, were suspects, including her.

Fiona's backpack was gone through. Satisfied, they gave it back to her.

Jack continued dictating the contact details to the cop, keeping half an eye on the interviews, halting to spell names that he, himself, had earlier asked to be spelled out.

Each interviewee in turn handed over their backpack for a quick search. The cops must be looking for the weapon, he thought. Surely, whoever had done it would not keep it. But they had to look.

Nova took a photo of each interviewee on her phone.

It was like a macabre doctor's waiting room, the walkers waiting for their interview. Once they had had their turn, they were told that they were free to go, but must come to Forest Gate Police Station tomorrow and give a full statement. It was impressed on them that this was a murder investigation and they had no choice in the matter. They were suspects. A jolt to hear such term from DI Kamani, Nova might have her authority questioned, but Kamani had a pukka warrant card, and the other cops under his command.

The walkers had left Forest Gate train station two hours ago, content and lively, with Mike as their leader. And now, he was dead and they were suspects in his murder.

Quite a change around.

Jack was the last to be interviewed, as it had taken some time for him to dictate all the details to the cop, who was a sluggish writer, and a poor speller. He kept saying slower, slower, give me that email again.

Kamani, the senior officer, went through Jack's backpack. He had water, the food he'd bought at the supermarket and nothing else. He was given the pack back, Kamani satisfied it contained no weapon.

Nova took his photograph.

'A mugshot for the family album,' she said, with a wry smile.

Jack was offered the free chair, Nova and Kamani were seated on the others. Crime scene tape ran past his shoulder. CSI had arrived and were scouring the scene beyond the tape, in full white coveralls, a mask over their mouths, only their eyes showing.

A high yellow tent was being put over the body. The police doctor in CSI gear, recognisable only by the bag he was carrying, was waiting for it to be erected, to give a little privacy for the corpse and his preliminary investigation.

'Strange place to meet, Jack,' said Detective Inspector Kamani.

'I would say, good to see you, Fayyad, but that doesn't feel right.'

'I'll take it as read, Jack.'

Nova was taking notes. She was the total cop, even without her warrant card, as if she didn't know him. Her bearing, her seriousness. But she had lost Mike, her lover, was that the right word? How far had they got, she and Mike, he wondered. What were they to each other? She didn't seem badly affected by his death, but that could be an act. Her job had taken over. She would weep later.

'How well did you know Mike Rayner?' said Fayyad.

'Today was the first time I'd met him. Didn't know his surname till you just said it. Penny invited me on the walk. I just knew her and you, Nova.'

'What did you think of him?' said Fayyad.

'Bossy. He had to be in charge.' Jack quoted in a gruff voice, 'Walk behind me. Snack break now. Who is leading this group, you or me!'

'When was the last time you saw him alive?'

'He got us together, told us to have a snack break while he went off to find the Witch's Tree.' Jack looked towards the tree with the erecting tent by its foot. 'Looks like he found it.'

'So you had the break, while he went off on his search,' said Kamani. 'Did you see any comings and goings?'

'No. I was busy. I'd bought a yogurt, but I didn't have a spoon.' He took the crumpled foil spoon out of his pocket. 'So I made one from scratch.' He straightened out the spoon. 'I got quite obsessed making it.' He laughed. 'Stupid thing really, but it worked. Took me some time to make. And then Penny joined me.'

Fayyad picked up the spoon, turned it over, showed it to Nova.

'It's not as easy as it looks,' said Jack. 'Not if you haven't made one before.'

'You say Penny joined you. Where had she been before that?'

Jack shrugged. 'No idea. I had my spoon to design and make, so I wasn't looking.' He stopped, looking from Nova to DI Kamani. 'Not a lot of help, am I?'

'Who knows what is of help?' said Kamani enigmatically.

'I saw Jack working on his spoon,' said Nova. 'Highly involved he was.'

'Am I a suspect?'

'Of course you are,' said Fayyad. 'All of you are.'

Jack thought of saying, what about the woman sitting next to you? But he didn't. Nova wasn't the killer. Then again, there were cops who were murderers. But not Nova. No way.

'I never knew the man,' said Jack. 'That surely rules me out.'

'So you say, but this job has made me suspicious of my own mother.'

'You weren't like that at school. How you have changed, Fayyad.' He snapped his fingers. 'Penny whistle. Fiona, the black woman, she was playing *When the Saints go Marching in*.'

'She told us.'

'A bit on the slow side, I thought.'

Fayyad smiled and rose. He put out his hand, he was one for shaking hands. Jack rose and shook his friend's hand.

'Bye, Jack. Thanks for your help. You may go. Don't forget to come into the station to make a statement tomorrow.'

'I'll be there. And bye, Nova.'

'See you, Jack.'

He wondered about that 'see you' as he left them. What did it mean? Something or nothing. We can be friends. Just words, habit, filler. Did he want them to be more?

The tent was now erected over the body. Presumably the doctor was inside it, but the front was closed to keep out prying eyes. Two of the CSI team were busy, creeping about the area, picking up odds and ends. There was a uniformed cop outside the crime tape where it crossed the trail to stop anyone coming through. And a second where it crossed again further up. A few onlookers were taking pictures with their phones. They could get no further than the tape where the duty cops offered them little information.

'A suspicious death,' they said to each request, 'I can't tell you any more.'

Jack was surprised to see Penny, the last of the walkers, seated on the ground against a tree, clearly waiting for him. She rose as he approached.

'Having invited you to this fiasco,' she said, 'I thought I should accompany you back to Forest Gate.'

'What should I read into that?' said Jack.

'That I am well mannered.'

Jack glanced behind him, Fayyad and Nova were still seated and talking, presumably comparing the statements of the walkers. Nova looked his way, then quickly turned back to her boss. Whether it was because he was with Penny, he couldn't say, but his heart gave a jump. He wasn't over her. Not the best of times to suggest another go. Mike might be out of the way, but she was grieving, and that left no room for him.

He and Penny set off for Forest Gate.

It was a grim walk back. A dead body reminds you of your own mortality. The shudder of it. Death could come early and suddenly, or be many years away, but it was inevitably coming. Mike had been very alive 90 minutes ago, suspecting nothing, having organised this walk from Forest Gate to Theydon Bois via the Witch's Tree. And then, his life was cut short.

Who knows, who knows when.

The sky had clouded over. It would not be a good night for astronomy, no stars or planets on view, just stratus cloud. The breeze had picked up, a sprinkling of leaves fluttered off the trees. Some way off, there were the cries from a football match. This was an ordinary Saturday afternoon with most people doing what they normally did at such times: shopping, football, housework, lounging around, on their phones, working in shops and cafes.

But a man had died, and they were suspects. Normality was suspended.

'I didn't know him, I didn't like him,' said Jack, out of nothing. 'Though I've been taught not to speak ill of the dead.'

'He can't hear you.'

'A hedge fund manager,' said Jack. 'Well-off pretty obviously. The latest phone, that was a watch on his wrist that could be put with the Crown Jewels. I wonder who gets his money.'

'He has a penthouse flat in Canary Wharf. I went there once. He had some fancy paintings, investments he called them, antique furniture. And clocks, old clocks. Quite a lot of them. One very weird one. A cuckoo grandfather clock. Out popped the cuckoo on the hour, quite shook me. And then, all the other clocks were chiming away, bings and bongs and little chimes. He used to wind them all up daily.'

'Why did you go to his flat?'

She smiled wryly. 'What are you suggesting?' She grinned. 'I'll put you right. Mike invited me back to his place after a walk, for a coffee, he said, and I was curious. He'd told me his flat had a marvellous view over the river. And it did. And yes, he tried it on. But I told him that I had just

46

come for coffee. No more.' She laughed. 'He made a good cup of coffee and we talked clocks. He opened a few up for me. I find them fascinating. Mechanical clocks, not the digital things. Pendulums and all the cogs, how energy is converted into a measure of time. More fascinating than he was.'

'Who do you think killed him?'

They had come to Lake House Road, the one where Mike, alive Mike, had stood holding back the traffic.

Once across, on the Flats again, she said:

'One of us did it, or someone else.'

'That's exactly what I said to Deneb. And he told me I was saying the obvious. Something like that.'

'Obvious, it may be. But that's where you start. Sure, he could have been killed by one of us. I won't evade that. Could be that one of us went to the Witch's Tree and went for him. The rip in his jacket, says he was stabbed in the back.'

'And whoever it was, then came back and ate their sandwiches,' added Jack.

'A couple of minutes is all you'd need. If you knew where you were going. You would have to be cool, to then join the others as if nothing has happened. Or there's the other option: not one of us. An email had been sent to everyone in the group informing us of today's walk. It told us where Mike was taking the walk, and that one of his stops was the Witch's Tree. M, I'll call him/her M for murderer. M knew the walk started at 10 am, and that Mike was a stickler for time, so it was easy for M to calculate how long it would take the group to get to the Witch's Tree, and to be there first.'

'So what do you reckon, one of us or someone else?'

'If I wanted to kill him, I wouldn't have gone on the walk. Or...' she laughed, ' have invited you.'

'If you, as the murderer, didn't go on the walk, you would run the risk of being spotted. The group knows you. So a big risk.'

'Risks either way,' she agreed.

The gulls were still there, the same or different ones, pecking at the thin grass recovering from the last funfair. There were a couple of dog walkers letting their animals run free. Never having had pets, Jack was always cagey with dogs, deciding whether to give them a wide berth or walk by them. Today, he took his cue from Penny. Though, maybe she was taking hers from him. Either way, two was more forceful if it came to a vicious dog.

He said, 'Someone else or M, but didn't have to be a walker. Could have been someone where he worked or someone he crossed in business. I am sure he could be cut-throat. Or a woman he treated badly or a clock dealer he refused to pay. Not just walkers.'

'Yes,' she said, 'could have been so many people. Except for one thing. Do you know what I am referring to?'

'The Witch's Tree.'

'Yes. Only our walking club knew that the tree was a stop on the way. The email details went round about two weeks ago, so plenty of time to recce it before today.'

He more or less agreed with her reasoning, meaning the killer was one of today's group or someone else in the club with a grudge against Mike. Today's group, he thought most likely, but it was a tricky hand to call.

They skirted a clump of gorse, which had, unseasonably, a few yellow flowers.

She said, 'I don't like being a suspect, Jack. I am a university professor. Quite respectable. Why would I want to murder him?'

'I could could come up with a scenario.'

'Go on. Something suitable for Hollywood.'

They were on the bumpy mole hills. Tricky to cross, you had to watch your feet, especially when talking.

'Mike invited you up to his flat, and then assaulted you,' said Jack. 'No clock talk.'

'Untrue.' She shook her head vehemently. 'He tried it on for sure, but I'm no teenage pushover. Clocks and coffee. That's all. What about you?'

'Me? I'd never met him before today.'

'So you say.'

'You invited me on the walk.'

'How lucky.' She squeezed her brow in contemplation. 'I think you and Nova plotted it together. Such a coincidence that I invited you, too.'

'I was making a spoon over the snack break!'

'You could have made one earlier. Like a Blue Peter demonstrator.' She put her hands up to signify peace. 'OK, OK, you are the least likely, I accept it, but you can't be ruled out completely. The unlikely can still happen.'

'I could win the lottery.'

'There you are. What's that? 15 million to one for a big win. Very unlikely, but not impossible.'

She put an arm on his shoulder and stopped him. They were mid-Flats, cawing crows and squawking gulls, blue patches appearing in the sky. In the distance, way across the middle road, they could see the colours of tiny football players, too far away to hear them on this odd Saturday.

'We could solve it,' she said. 'If it's one of the group.'

'How?'

'Go and see everyone tomorrow. Sunday. Pretend they are helping us solve it. And question them.' She clapped her hands. 'A pair of sleuths! I'll pick you up at ten tomorrow morning, and we'll visit them one at a time.'

'I do have all the addresses and contact details...' he said warily. Not totally convinced that it was an OK activity.

'Perfect. Come on, Jack. You told me you were setting up as a detective. Well, here's an investigation on your doorstep. What do you say, Sherlock?'

'I think you have caught me on my weak spot. I can't say no.'

'What a gent!' She hugged him mid-Flats. And they homed in for a kiss, forgetting for a minute the killing they were both suspects for.

Chapter 8

Back at his flat, Penny had popped in for a coffee, they discussed how to go about the interviews tomorrow. She would phone everyone up to set up the times.

'I am not staying long,' she said. 'Not a good idea, so early in our relationship. Too soon.' She was distracted by his telescope, in the corner of his sitting room.

'The 150 millimetre parabolic reflector,' she said, and went for a closer look.

Jack was always happy to talk about his scope. It's a bit hefty, he told her. But he put it in his wheelbarrow, he said, when he went stargazing on the Flats.

'You could come some time,' he said.

'I'd like that.'

They embraced, and she left. She'd be over tomorrow at 10 am to pick him up for the interviews, if everyone was agreeable.

On his own, Jack put the kettle back on. Tea this time, more his drink. No need to cook, he still had the food that he'd bought in the morning for the walk. No yogurt, and he'd eaten the banana on the walk back, but he still had a packet of crisps and the pack of four energy bars.

Jack put them on the table as he made himself a cup of tea. He had a small teapot, just the size for one. Mia had bought him it for his birthday a year or two back, and he preferred it to dunking a teabag in a cup. More civilised.

So, he and Penny had agreed to do some detective work. That chuffed him, a professor thinking he was good enough. But good enough meant finding out who the killer was in the group, if it was indeed one of the group. Though, it had occurred to him, even as she was making the suggestion of sleuthing, that Penny could be the killer. She was confident, cool, calculating.

If so, why would she want to play detective? To muddy the waters perhaps, to find out what the others had on her. The killer needed just a few minutes, he and she had agreed, so had Penny left the group for that long? Did anyone notice?

The kettle had boiled, and he poured the hot water into his little teapot, just as the flat door opened.

'Hi, Dad!'

Mia appeared at the kitchen door and flung her blue anorak on the sitting room sofa. Her mum would tell her off for that, but Jack did the same himself, so he could hardly complain.

His daughter was almost his height, with wild, dark brown curls, casually dressed in blue jeans and a green sweat top, and trainers that she'd almost walked to death.

'There's hot water in the kettle,' he said.

She made herself a cup of tea and sat down with her father at the table, taking one of his energy bars.

'You're back early from your walk,' she said.

Jack had spoken to her last night on the phone, telling her about his computer date, which Mia was ultra curious about, and Penny's invitation to a 13 mile walk from Forest Gate to Theydon Bois.

'The walk got interrupted quite early on,' he said, wondering how to put it, even as he spoke. 'Do you know the Witch's Tree?'

She pulled the teabag out of her mug and dropped it in the bin.

'Sure. That tree over Bushwood, across the Flats. The one they say wanders in the night. The raised roots look like spider legs. When I was a kid, I used to crawl through it. What about it?'

'The walk leader got murdered by the side of it.'

'You are joking.' She was agog. 'Do tell!'

Having begun with such a downplayed line, he needed to give the full tale. Beginning with the rendezvous at Forest Gate station, and finding Nova there, as well as Penny, to complicate his love life. He told her about bossy Mike, and how he couldn't find the Witch's Tree. That made sense to Mia, as sometimes she and her mum found it tricky to find, and went back and forth till they did. And then the preamble to finding the body, the snack break. Making a spoon from a yogurt foil top.

From his pocket, Jack brought out the squished spoon, pressing it out to give it some semblance of its once practical usage.

But his daughter waved it away.

'Forget the spoon. And stop spinning it out.'

He rolled his eyes, pushing down his disappointment that she had dismissed his ingenuity. On with the tale, it had to be filled out, or it wasn't a tale worth telling. They had searched for Mike, listening out for the ringtone. Until they found him, splayed out dead by the Witch's Tree.

'You only walked about two miles,' she said.

'And back again.'

He could see she was shocked, under that bravado. Who wouldn't be?

'So who do you think is the killer?' She picked up a second energy bar, then put it down. 'These are not good for you, you know. Way too much sugar.' She got up and brought her own backpack over. 'You never buy fruit and veg, even though it's doctor's orders.'

She opened her backpack and put oranges, bananas, broccoli and French beans on the table.

'Me and Penny are investigating,' he said ignoring the healthy additions.

'Getting on so quickly. Suppose she's the killer.'

'Then I'll break up the partnership.'

'You might be dead.'

'I shall be careful.'

She harrumphed. 'Like you always are.'

'Are you here for the weekend? Or just for an annoying hour.'

'Mum and I had a big row.'

'Another one?' It was a regular feature of Mia's life. 'Over what?'

'I'm leaving school. She says she won't let me. I told her she can't stop me. Anyway, I've come here for a few days. School's out. I'll help you with the detective agency. Any work come in?'

'I haven't looked online, but I doubt there's anything. Besides, I'll be busy finding Mike's killer.'

'That's amateur stuff. Dating really. Paid work is what you need. I'll work on your website. And I want a cut of any income.'

'20% of nothing, well why not make it 50?'

'You would regret that,' she said, 'when you're working for me. But I won't take advantage. So, tell me some more about this Penny, now she's going to feature in your life. I liked Nova sometimes, but couldn't get over the fact she was a cop. So, Penny's CV?'

'Can we go back a step. You said you are leaving school?' She nodded. 'Why?'

'It's irrelevant.' She threw out her arms to indicate how little it mattered. 'Climate change is in the driving seat. I don't need any more education, I need to get out on the streets.'

'And your mother isn't happy.'

'Doubly unhappy.' She smirked. 'She wants me to stay at school and cut out the demos.'

'I'll talk to her,' he said.

'You won't change my mind.'

PART TWO:
IN THE SHOP

Chapter 9

The next morning, Jack was up at 9 ish. He'd wanted a fry up but Mia had made him a disappointingly healthy breakfast: muesli with banana and bits of orange. He ate it, but it just seemed to lack substance. No meat hit.

Mia was at the kitchen table with him. She held up the milk carton.

'Time to stop buying this.'

He didn't say anything but waited for the sermon.

'Cows have to be pregnant,' she said, 'to keep giving milk. But when the calves are born, farmers don't want them as calves need their mothers' milk. So economics dictates mass slaughter, hundreds of thousands of calves every year.' She held up the carton. 'There's blood in this.'

'You sure know how to spoil a good breakfast. Not a lot one can eat. Bacon comes from pigs crammed into sheds, eggs from battery chickens.'

'We buy free range, if that makes you tell better.'

'Now tell me why I shouldn't.'

'Male chicks don't lay eggs. So they are killed soon after hatching. Gassed usually. As they are no good for meat either, there's two sound reasons to gas male chicks.' She rubbed her hands together in a mercenary manner. 'Capitalist economics.'

'Thank God for muesli,' he said. She could go on and on, working to put him off meat, milk, eggs and anything animal-born. 'What are you up to today?'

'Prettying up your website. Giving it some oomph. If we want customers, they have to believe we can deliver.'

Jack noted the 'we', but fair enough. The detective agency didn't exist until they got a customer. But he was half intrigued and half in dread of what she might come up with, giving his website some oomph. Claiming, no doubt, he was the Philip Marlowe of the East End. Though, he doubted Lauren Bacall would show up.

Penny phoned on the dot of 10 am. She was outside in her car. Jack was ready and grabbed his coat. Mia came down with him to take a look at 'the professor he'd pulled'.

But the professor was a little way up the road in her vehicle, so Mia could get barely a glimpse.

'Catch the killer,' she said grumpily, 'so I can give you some all singing, all dancing copy.'

He kissed her on the cheek, there was no point asking her to lower expectations. And went out to Penny, feeling a little fluttery. Professors were daunting. He must stop seeing her as one. In fact, she was dressed much as she was yesterday, the same red coat, but no woolly hat or boots but sensible flat shoes.

She held open the car door, and kissed him on the cheek once he was seated. He hoped Mia wasn't watching. Kids, even grown up ones, can curtail one's love life. Kill it dead.

'I've set up three appointments,' she said. 'Fiona was busy, although she can do Tuesday evening.'

She had used the contact details Jack had collected. And had phoned the walkers last night. No point Jack helping out with that. She was a regular walker, while he was hardly known to them, just a newbie who came on yesterday's truncated outing.

'I flattered them,' said Penny, 'saying I knew it couldn't possibly be them, but we, emphasising the 'we', with our collective brain power should work out who was the guilty party.' She smiled, enjoying her guile.

Again Jack wondered, if it might be her? As if being a professor was not bad enough.

They drove down to East Ham. The borough where Jack lived, the London borough of Newham, to give it its full title, was created in 1965, when the two boroughs of East Ham and West Ham were combined into a larger borough, in which much energy and argument was expended, before coming up with the name Newham, which had long ago lost its newness, and the final 'a' in its pronunciation.

They might have gone in his van, of course, but with *Jack of All Trades* painted on both sides, it was somewhat conspicuous, as much his tool shed as transport.

Penny didn't need her satnav. Too local a journey. She headed down to the Romford Road, which was fairly quiet on a Sunday morning. Not so Green Street which she turned into, a well known Asian shopping street replete with sari shops, emporiums, jewellers, Indian restaurants and food shops. And too much traffic.

Frustrated being stuck behind a bus, Penny turned off down a side road, but even this wasn't easy to navigate with cars parked on both sides. Motorist had to squeeze past oncoming motorists, deciding who should stop and who should go, with impatient hooting and gestures, before one car gave in and backed up.

It was warmish for October, quite sunny, not too much cloud in a largely blue sky. Might be a good night for a telescope outing but he'd decide his options later, depending how today went with Penny.

She gave in to her satnav, not wanting to be caught out by the one-way system at East Ham. And so followed, the polite, imperious, received pronunciation of the very English woman, who might have been minor royalty born on horseback, but was more likely a computer creation.

They turned onto the Barking Road, busy with buses and cars, heading into London in one direction and out to Barking and Essex in the other. Where do they all go on a Sunday morning? They can't all be hunting killers. Penny was an impatient driver, swearing even, which quite surprised him. On building sites every other word was a profanity, but not professors surely, though his experience was limited. To one.

They turned down High Street South at the old town hall, passing a lesser known Central Park, keeping an eye out for somewhere to leave the car.

Phil lived in a third floor flat in a five story block on the main road. They walked up to the third floor, not trusting the lift, via a miasma of urine on the concrete stairwell, and continuing along the external balcony. Penny rang the doorbell.

He answered promptly, smiled at seeing Penny, then switched off at seeing Jack.

'Why is he here?' he exclaimed.

Phil was dressed in exactly the same clothes as yesterday. Maybe he slept in them. A musty smell exuded from his hallway, as if he didn't open his windows at all. The hallway was crowded with framed paintings, piles of books, and cardboard boxes with heaven knows what inside, leaving an alley hardly body-sized to negotiate.

But they weren't invited in. Phil stood across the door, like a bouncer outside a nightclub.

Penny said, 'I thought, as Jack is an innocent party, he hadn't met Mike before yesterday, and is unprejudiced, he be a good one to have along.'

'I'm a builder,' said Jack, though quite how that would assist in placating Phil's doubts, he wondered even as he said the words. Plough on.

'I've got a feel for people,' he added. 'I can tell you are genuine, Phil. You say it as it is. An honest East Ender.'

Flattery usually worked, he'd found with customers. His own brand of dishonesty. It shouldn't work, too obvious. But Phil smiled broadly.

'Welcome aboard,' said Phil. 'No wokery, eh?'

Jack didn't know what Phil branded as wokery, but he was here to be agreeable.

'No wokery,' he said.

Phil put out his hand and they shook.

'I was thinking of going up to The Miller's Well,' said Phil.

They would have rather have gone inside his flat, never mind the smell and its crowded state, as a home gives the feel of the occupant. And you never know what you might see. Then again, a drink or two might add to Phil's verbiage.

Jack tried to avoid pubs in the usual run of things, now he was on the wagon. Avoid the danger spots, said Max, his mentor. But this wasn't his call. For an hour on a Sunday morning, he could hold out from his former addiction.

So they settled for the pub, as it was their function to keep Phil talking, as, anytime he chose, Phil could call a halt to the proceedings.

Chapter 10

The Miller's Well, up from the old town hall on the Barking Road, was a Victorian pub enhanced by a Wetherspoon's makeover. At 10.30 on a Sunday morning, it was fairly quiet.

They found a cubicle. And Jack went off to get the drinks, having ascertained what they wanted. He, himself, would go for a non-alcoholic beer, where, at least, it would appear he was drinking alcohol and supporting Phil. The name of the game, all mates together, to keep him talking.

When he returned with the tray of beverages, Penny and Phil were chatting away about walks coming up. Surprising in the view of what happened yesterday, but life on earth goes on, even as another passes on to a disputable domain.

Thanking Jack, they took their drinks.

'Lovely,' said Phil, slapping his lips after his first mouthful. 'I do like an Old Speckled Hen. Greene King, you know. What's that you're drinking, Jack?'

He had to admit it was non-alcoholic, saying he'd had a heavy session last night. Penny was on fruit juice, as she was driving.

'You know why we are here,' she said, getting down to business.

Phil took a long sip. 'To keep me in beer.' He laughed, took another sip, adding, 'You want to find the killer. Me too.'

'We thought you, being an old member, with no gripe against Mike,' said Penny, 'would have some insight on who killed him.'

'Someone on the walk for starters,' said Phil. 'Who did we have?' He enumerated them on his chubby fingers.

'Fiona, the black woman who plays the penny whistle and had a cat called Marcus Garvey. What a name for an animal. I had a row with her over Alice in Wonderland, would you believe? Then we had Liz who is a West Ham season ticket holder, no wonder she's always so miserable,' he chuckled and then took another sip. 'And Nova – the cop who lied to us, saying she worked for the Council.'

'You have quite a memory,' said Jack. This, at least, was true. He was impressed that Phil recalled their headlines as they went round the circle on the edge of the Flats yesterday.

Obviously flattered, Phil continued. 'You, Penny, were born a year after Halley's Comet came round.'

She smiled at his remembrance.

'And something about prime numbers, I can't remember what.' He held up a hand to stop her telling him. 'That Asian guy, Deneb, he crossed the Channel in a crowded rubber dinghy.' He tapped his head with a finger. 'I may like my drink, but I've still got all my little grey cells.'

'Who killed Mike?' said Penny, keeping him to the point.

'One of the group, that's for sure,' he said. 'Not you two, so that doesn't leave many. I'd rule out the cop, Nova. So that leaves Fiona, Liz and Deneb. Now Fiona is a cow. I hate her and her woke attitudes, but she wouldn't kill Mike because he annoyed her. And he would big time as she doesn't like the rich, being something of a commie. I'd like it to be her, but I bet it isn't.'

'What about Deneb and Anne?' said Penny.

'That Deneb, he's a quiet one. An asylum seeker. I'm not anti boat people, but some of them came out of war zones. Learned to kill, had to in order to survive. Who knows what he got up to?'

'But why would he kill Mike?' said Jack.

'There you have me,' he went on. Phil put his empty glass down. 'Such a good pint.'

'I'll get 'em in,' said Penny. She rose and went off to the bar.

When she was out of earshot, Jack said, 'You've ruled out Penny? For definite?'

'What, you think she might have?' Phil laughed and nudged Jack in the ribs. 'Watch yourself, mate. You might wake up with a knife in your ribs.'

It had occurred to him. Though she wouldn't kill for bad sex, would she?

'What would be her motive?' said Jack.

'She went out with Mike for a short while. That's all I can tell you. What happened in his penthouse... did you know he had a penthouse? I have no idea why she'd do it. But sex and money, the evil twins. What else is there?' Phil laughed, taking another sip, enjoying the beer and being the centre of attraction.

'Religion,' said Jack, adding a few more motivators. 'Machismo, flag-waving, racism, insanity, which could include any of the others or none of them...'

Phil flapped away the added motives. 'I'd still go for sex and money. Maybe both. Mike liked his sex, had plenty of dosh, too much some would say.'

He was looking across to the bar, eyes lighting up at seeing Penny on the way back with a tray of drinks. Arriving, she put the tray on the table. The same all round: Old Speckled Hen, fruit juice, and non-alcoholic beer.

'Been talking about me behind my back, have you?' she said, as she sat down.

'Phil rules you out,' said Jack.

'And you?'

She was looking him in the eye. He felt a shudder and would have kissed her if Phil was not here, whether she was a killer or not.

'I can't think why you would,' he said. Which was true enough, but he didn't rule her out.

Phil was already working on his pint. Jack sipped his, hardly fancying it. No bite, like a vegetarian breakfast.

'Liz is devious,' said Phil, 'she's got secrets alright. You don't know what Liz is really thinking. She nods away but you know she believes the opposite. Would she kill?' He shrugged. 'Well, she's an ex social worker, I've met some, can be hard as nails. Take kids from decent homes, put them in care. Not that I know any of that about her, but she's on the wokey side. And even a Hammers fan would have to have a motive. And frankly, Mike went for good lookers. Not old crocks with skinny pins. Ones he could dress up and buy jewellery for. Someone his age or younger. That's money for you. Brings 'em in. It's sexy.'

'Not everyone liked Mike,' said Penny. 'But you did.'

'Sure, I liked him. Quite a show-off, but you can forgive that. He led a lot of walks which is more than you can say of other people. The club needs walk leaders. That's how we work. But there's too many moaners who never lead a walk. Yes, he had standards but if you don't like them, then don't come on his walks. Or lead a walk yourself with your wokey rules.'

'He was well off,' said Jack. 'Could've bought the lot of us, twice over.'

'Wealthy is the word,' said Phil. 'And Mike flaunted it alright, with his Rolex watch, Ray-Ban sunglasses, the latest iPhone. Everyone should have a good watch, he told me once. Which I thought a bit crackers as my phone tells me the time to a thousandth of a second. So why do I need a poncy watch? Just status, am I right?' He looked to them for confirmation.

'On the button,' said Jack. 'As usual.'

'Then again,' went on Phil, 'you have to accept there are rich people in the world, and, really, what's the point of money if you don't flaunt it.'

Phil took a long drink as if he was behind schedule. And maybe he was, just a pint and half drunk and much of the morning gone. He put the glass down, licked his lips.

'That Old Speckled Hen is really something. Where was I?'

'You were telling us Mike was rich,' prompted Penny.

'I used to joke with him about being a hedge fund manager. Buy shrubs, do you? Making lots of lolly out of holly.' He laughed at his own wit. 'Hedge funds, whatever they are, just another way of robbing the poor, if you ask me. But the thing about the rich is that they buy art. Well, the poor can't afford to. And Mike, he bought a painting of mine. Paid well. More than I thought it was worth. I named a price, thought he would bargain me down, but he accepted it there and then. But something is worth what someone will pay for it. That's the art world. Us artists, if I can call myself such, we need people who buy art. So I liked him, thought him a show off, but he had his good qualities.'

'We never thought you killed him,' said Penny. 'Ruled you out from the off.'

'And Christmas is coming,' said Jack, looking at his watch. Not a Rolex, but twenty quid ten years ago, and kept decent time. All the fuss about watches, he agreed, was bonkers.

Christmas was their signal to leave. Another pint, and Phil would just say the same things over and over. Or different things as he muddled his way through the morning.

Chapter 11

They headed west, along the Barking Road, which would morph into, once over the Canning Town flyover, the East India Dock Road, and then Commercial Road, passing by the two river tunnels, Blackwall and Rotherhithe, out to the City, its iconic skyscrapers on the horizon.

'So what do you think?' she said, en route. 'Could it be Phil?'

'Sex wouldn't be a motive, though you never know, but I reckon money ticks his box. I worked for this rich couple once. They loved what I did to their kitchen, a full makeover, I had to strip it all out, all new stuff in. They said they'd recommend me to their friends. I was in debt at the time, so this was wonderful, a promise from heaven.'

'Don't tell me. They didn't tell anyone.'

'They went off to the Bahamas. I was gutted, hoping for rich customers, bigger jobs.' He stopped and shook his head. 'The rich make promises, and then forget what they have said. Just words to them, a way of saying goodbye.'

'You think Mike might have made promises to Phil. About his paintings.'

'He said he'd sold one to Mike. I reckon Phil doesn't have many customers. So he would be sending Mike pictures of his latest. Weekly. And getting back, teasing words.'

'Better if Mike had never bought any at all,' she mused.

They were approaching the Canning Town flyover, a concrete arch over the River Lea, taking you from Newham into the London borough of Tower Hamlets.

There used to be a music pub nearby. Quite famous. What was it called? He snapped his fingers.

'The Bridge House! Used to be here,' he expounded. 'Got knocked down for the flyover. Old rockers still talk about it. U2 were there, Annie Lennox, Dire Straits, Iron Maiden, Tom Robinson. Destroyed to build that concrete monstrosity.' He was aware he was sounding like his daughter, with her diatribe on concrete's contribution to climate change.

'Not a good swap,' she agreed. 'Let's park.'

Liz lived up on the 17th floor of a tower block overlooking the flyover and Canning Town station. The block had a concierge at a desk in a carpeted vestibule. The lift was much choicer than Phil's would have been, if they had taken his. It was mirrored and smooth running, with a frontage of glass, lifting them high into the sky, with views over the river and the Millennium Dome in its armpit. A temporary building built to boast of the UK's art and technology, ridiculed by the chattering classes, but still around, a quarter of century later.

Her flat wasn't large, but was tidy, the furniture choice and newish. The view not riverside.

'It shaved off 10 thou if I didn't go for a river view,' she said, 'allowing me to jettison my old furniture, and be more minimalist.' She gestured around. 'Some of the old stuff went to the British Heart Foundation shop in Ilford, and some they wouldn't take. It was sad, I couldn't even give away my sofa. Well, I suppose I could have, but how? A couple of people came to see it. Too big. Not worth the transport.'

She'd been here five years, Liz told them, moving from Ilford, just about affording one of the small flats with the sale of her house.

'With the girls gone, I didn't need three bedrooms. Gill is in Spain, Ellie in Australia.' She indicated the photos around, on the walls and on the sideboard, of her daughters, their spouses and her grand children. 'I do miss them,' she said with a sigh, 'but I get no say on where they go. Nor should I.'

When they were seated with coffee and biscuits, they got going, the schedule was tight.

'What did you think of Mike,' said Penny. Her coat was on a chair, revealing a yellow jumper, with an ancient Greek goddess throwing a javelin. Artemis, she had told him.

'I thought Mike was rather up himself,' said Liz. 'Do you know, he wore a five thousand pound watch on a walk or was it ten thousand? Hardly matters. So stupid! On a walk!' She leaned forward, appalled. 'I asked him why, and he told me it was his second best watch. As if that was any sort of answer, I mean, it's like walking around with a big note saying *steal me*! And to think, the price of it could house a homeless family. But he didn't care.'

'But you still went on his walks,' said Penny.

'His walks were OK. Well, you know yourself. So long as you don't have to talk to him. Just stay well behind him. Mind you, he did his research, so you got history as you went along. I'm into history so that's a plus. Too many didn't like him which is why there were only eight of us on Saturday. I do consider who is leading. But sometimes, it's the only walk going, so you go, even if you are not keen on the leader. I don't like long, fast walks. Maybe ten years ago, but you have to accept your age, and how it slows you down.'

'Who do you think killed him?' said Jack.

Coffee and biscuits were nice mid morning, but it was time for the big questions.

'I don't know,' she shrugged. 'Mike was rich, that was obvious with all that gear. Hedge fund manager, whatever that is. He was abrasive, made enemies and didn't seem to care. Reckoned his money kept him out of the melee. Wrong there, wasn't he? He didn't keep girlfriends long.' She turned to Penny. 'You went out with him a couple of time, didn't you?'

'Soon found out he wasn't my type,' she said. 'Too controlling.'

Jack took another shortbread biscuit, and hoped no one was counting. And he mustn't be too controlling. Though, he had the feeling, it would be Penny who'd call the shots, if this relationship had any traction.

'I was surprised at Nova going out with him,' Liz went on. 'But he was good looking. I can't tell you what he was like in bed,' she grinned, 'but he flashed his money around, and that pulled them in. Never saw him without a girlfriend for long.'

'At the snack break yesterday,' said Penny, 'can you tell us about comings and goings?

'Exactly what the cops asked me. But as I told them, I wasn't watching out. I mean, who knew I needed to. I saw Phil go off for a pee break. He drinks a fair bit. Has a big flask, he says it's apple juice, apple juice smapple juice. And me, I went off into the woods for a pee myself. I spotted some mushrooms, I know a bit about them, it's the time of year for fungi. Fly agaric, those spotty red umbrellas gnomes sit on. I took some photos, I'll show you if you want. As I came back, I could hear the penny whistle. I thought who is that. Never heard it before. It was Fiona. I got talking to her about that stupid row with Phil over a black Alice. Don't know what Nova was up to, though I did see her wandering around with her phone talking to someone. I didn't know she was a cop. I suppose you keep that stuff dark. She said she worked for the Council. Would you call that a white lie?'

'Did you kill him?' said Penny.

That was a blast too soon. Liz recoiled.

'Are you joking?' she said.

'Yes,' Penny. 'I think so.'

'So maybe, it's not a joke.'

'I thought it needed to get to be got out into the open,' said Penny. She shrugged. 'Aren't we all suspects?'

Liz glared at her.

'Why would I kill him? Because he's sexist? Well, I'd have to kill half the population, wouldn't I? Because he's rich? How would that help me? I had no reason to kill him. I didn't like him, but so what? On a walk, it's easy to avoid people.'

'What do you do apart from walk?' said Jack.

Her eyes screwed up. 'Why are you asking me all this?'

She looked from one to the other and took a deep intake of breath, as if realising.

'I know you are a West Ham fan,' said Jack, knowing they'd overstepped the mark. 'Me too. I go to a couple of games a season. When I get paid. Seats are pricey.'

Hoping to placate her with football.

'I know what you two are up to.' She looked from one to the other, teeth gritted. 'Detectives, amateur sleuths. The cops are already on to this. They don't need two clumsy gumshoes.'

'Sorry if we've offended you, Liz,' said Penny. 'It's just that we hate being suspects. And feel, well maybe, we can clear it up...'

'Better than the cops. Huh?'

'Quicker than the cops,' said Jack.

'By treating everyone as suspects, except your blessed selves. Shall I ask you about your lives? Whether you killed him? Did you stick a knife in him, Penny?'

'I apologise, Liz. I had no wish to offend you.'

'Well, you are way past that. I am well and truly offended. But for completeness, I shall answer your last question. Your very last. What do I do apart from walk. So here's me in a nutshell, you cloth-eared Sherlocks. I've a season ticket for West Ham. My one big luxury. I go to West Ham home games.' She hammered the answers as if into a door she wanted to break down. 'I volunteer in a charity shop for disabled people two days a week. I'm retired, I was a social worker for 35 years. I go to Spain at least once a year to see my daughter. I read a lot, and belong to a book group. I've got a good friend in Basildon who I talk to most days. We go to the theatre together sometimes, go on walks together. Sometimes sleep together. It's why my marriage went phut, but I was only too glad to see the back of the bastard.' She stopped, seething with anger. 'Now, clear off and accuse someone else of murder.'

Chapter 12

They sat in the car, shell-shocked.

'That went well,' he said.

'A classic example of how not to conduct an interview.'

'Don't ask a lady if she's a killer. Unless you're a cop.'

They didn't speak for a while. She was resting her head on the steering wheel, while he lay back, instinctively looking at the sky, watching the movement of the clouds.

'Liz could be guilty,' said Penny. 'Hence, her extreme reaction.'

'Liz could be innocent,' said Jack. 'Hence, her extreme reaction.'

'I just wonder,' said Penny, 'all that anger. Was the lady protesting too much?'

'She sure bundled us out. And slammed the door in our faces.'

'No one died,' she said.

'At least, not today.'

'I deserved her brickbats,' said Penny. 'I lied to get the interview, like a tabloid journalist. I told her I knew that she wasn't the murderer, when I have no idea whether she is or isn't.'

'So what do we do, Miss Marple?'

Penny blew out her cheeks, and shook her hands in frustration. 'I bet you, Liz will be emailing the others, telling them what these – what did she call us?'

'Cloth-eared Sherlocks.'

'I had a teacher who once call me cloth-eared. I know it's an insult but I'm not too sure what it means.'

'Stupid, daft.'

'But why cloth?' She waved a hand. 'Don't answer. It's off piste, whether our ears are cloth or fleshy.'

'Quite nice with those earrings.' She wore a gold ring in each. 'And I am sure they don't make you stupid.'

'Go away. No, stay!'

She squeezed his hand.'

'So what do we do?' he said.

'Deneb will know we are a pair of pseuds if he gets her message. I laid it on with a trowel when I spoke to him last night.'

'I have the feeling he won't care very much.'

'Why?'

'He's an outsider. Deneb is used to not being trusted. The Home Office assumes everyone is lying, especially if you come off a sunken dinghy.'

She thought about this, as if it were an equation that wouldn't quite work out. 'He either won't let us in. Or he will. Either way, we are not any worse off. Might get Liz out of our system.' She paused, something had struck her. 'She said she has two daughters. Could one of them have been involved with Mike?'

'That's a long shot. You're the mathematician. What's the odds?'

'Insufficient data.'

'Was Mike abusive?'

She was quiet a while, obviously troubled. Then said:

'He could be. The need for control. I got out quickly, but someone who was more vulnerable...'

'A slim possibility, let's say, one of her daughters,' he said.

'Slim is not zero.'

'I think we should see Deneb,' he said. 'Be straight with him. Tell him, we don't know who the killer is.'

'Sometimes, you are quite smart,' she said.

'And sometimes?'

'I don't know. I'll tell you when I know you better.'

She kissed him on the nose, and before he could react, turned on the engine.

Chapter 13

Deneb lived in Stratford, on a short road between one of the Bow back rivers and the Greenway, a publicist's name for the covered sewage pipes that traversed from Stratford down to the Beckton Sewage plant, the largest such works in Europe. The Greenway pipes were grassed over, with a concrete central track along its three mile length, beloved by cyclists, popular with walkers, though from time to time, from the various manholes one had a whiff of its real purpose.

They pulled up before a row of terraced Victorian houses.

'Honesty our watchword,' said Jack.

'As the day is young,' vowed Penny.

They punched fists. Jack took a deep breath as they exited the vehicle.

'Let's hope this goes better,' he said.

'Could hardly be worse.'

They rang the bell, and in a few seconds could hear footsteps coming down stairs. Deneb opened up.

'Hello, Penny, hello, Jack. So nice to see you. Please come in.'

Deneb had the top floor of the house. A bicycle hung from hooks just past the internal flat door. As they climbed the stairs, he said, 'I've bought a cake for you.'

He took them into the sitting room at the front of the house, a medium sized room, with a two person sofa and an armchair. There was a bookshelf, half full. A sideboard, with a lone framed photo on top, of a woman and a boy about six years old. There was a small wooden table with two chairs by the window. The room was carpeted. It didn't seem at all like the room of a man from the Middle East.

'None of this furniture is mine,' he said, seeing them looking about. 'The house is owned by Queen Mary University, the college at Mile End. They are my employers and have a few properties which they rent to staff. I was so lucky to get this place. It's impossible to find somewhere decent to live in London. This is so convenient. I cycle into work. It's just a couple of miles up the Bow Road. Please excuse me, I am neglecting my duties. I'll make some tea. I don't often have guests.'

He left them and they looked around the room. It had the odour of loneliness.

'One photo,' said Penny.

Jack nodded. It was the one personal touch in the room. The few things Deneb had had with him went down in the Channel, along with the people in the photograph. How did he get the photo? Jack looked at it closely. It was blurry.

'A copy of an online photo,' said Penny. 'Maybe Facebook.'

The room silenced them. They couldn't talk about the investigation. It would have sounded conspiratorial, as they could hear the clinking china in the nearby kitchen, and so would likely be heard.

'Read any good books lately,' she said, jokily, not expecting it to be taken up.

'*Magnetic Earth*,' he said to confound her. 'It's about the earth as a magnet, with solid iron in the centre, liquid iron surrounding it, with all the currents in the fluid, giving the earth its magnetic field which wards off the sun's cosmic rays.'

She laughed. 'Are those your usual chat up lines?'

'You did ask,' he said, a little offended. 'I'm not good at small talk,' he said. 'The weather and where I went on my holidays, that stuff. Is that what you'd rather hear?'

'Actually, I prefer talk about the earth's magnetic field, to the usual chat up guff.'

'It's my test,' he said. 'If you have no interest in the earth's magnetism or the formation of Saturn's rings, then we are not compatible.'

'I can see why there's no queue. Usually, it's qualities like good sense of humour or likes movies.'

'I'm choosy,' he said.

Deneb came in rattling a full tray which he placed on the table by the window. It had a teapot, three mugs, a milk jug, a sugar bowl, small mismatched plates and a large cream cake on a paper doily on a large plate.

'I so seldom have guests,' he said. 'I am not the best of hosts. I don't know what to say. Small talk, you call it.'

'Jack was saying, he's the same way. And was trying to interest me in the earth's magnetic field.'

Deneb beamed. 'I could talk about that. Probably say far too much. The poles could reverse any time, you know, but no one seems concerned. But that could be terrible time, when the south magnetic pole becomes the north and north becomes south, with the breakdown of the magnetic field in the polar regions. Cosmic rays would rain down on us, breaking down electronic communication, in fact anything electronic and causing mass cancers.' He stopped, 'Not a cheerful thought. The reversal of the poles are overdue, so could be next year, or in five hundred years time. The mathematics of prediction breaks down with such a chaotic system as the liquid iron swilling in the earth's centre.'

'Above the solid iron core,' Jack felt compelled to add.

'Once again, I am impressed with your knowledge, Jack.'

He handed rounds mugs of milkless tea and came to them both with the jug, adding the amount they required. Both declined sugar, but accepted cake.

Deneb took the armchair once he had given them cake.

'Thank you for agreeing to see us,' said Penny. 'I wasn't quite truthful in my earlier conversation with you.'

He waved away the necessity for excuses.

'I know we are all suspects, Penny,' he said. 'For all you know, I might have killed Mike. And similarly, you two.

Though, one should not say such things to guests, but it is so. So please don't apologise.'

'Thank you so much,' said Penny.

For his part, Jack was glad, they wouldn't begin the interview with a row. Or endless excuses.

'What did you think of Mike,' said Penny.

And so they began. Munching cake, sipping tea, as they interviewed their polite host.

'He wanted things done his way and only his way,' said Deneb, a little cream from the cake on his chin. *'Don't get ahead of me, I am right, always right, don't contradict me, look at my amazing watch.* It would be hell being married to him, I am sure. He had a lot of girlfriends. Whether they grew tired of him or he of them, I don't know. I've been in the club about a year, and been on some of his walks. I know quite a few people are annoyed by him. He always has new things: phone, expensive watch, boots, Goretex jacket. Always something, as if he has too much money and doesn't know what to do with it all.'

He took a sip of tea to refresh his thoughts.

'Mike didn't approve of me,' he continued. 'I am one of those labelled 'boat people', those awful people come to scrounge off the true Brits, as if that is all I am. I got into the country before those coming across the Channel, in those awful boats, were made illegal. Crazy laws. Illegal to cross the channel in a crowded boat, pushed on board by men with guns.'

He was silent for perhaps half a minute, as if enveloped in the nightmare of his Channel crossing. They waited on him, not wishing to intrude.

'On one of his walks,' he at last went on, 'Mike told me the country was too crowded. Enough is enough, he said. A nonsensical phrase. What else could enough be but enough? An uncomfortable conversation. He was one of those people who wanted to keep England for what he regarded as the English. Quite a restricted group. WASPs, they say in America.'

'You are a physicist,' said Penny, 'where did you study?'

'In Damascus for my degree and post graduate work, then I did two years at the University of California, Berkeley campus. I learnt a lot there, English as well as physics. I specialise in particle physics, wrote a number of papers. I was doing well. Then I went back to Syria, became a professor at Damascus University. I got married, we had a child, a boy, Ibrahim. Then the war started. Me and most of the students wanted to get rid of Assad, to have a democratic Syria. More fool me. When the Russians sided with Assad, I knew we would be overrun. We had to flee, get across the border while it was still open. That was a hellish time. Bribery, bribery, bribery. Everyone wanted your money, to cross a border, to not shoot you, to give you permits.'

It was if he were no longer with them in the room, but being ferried from country to country, unwanted in any of them.

'We travelled in the back of a lorry across Europe with more than 30 others and got dumped in Calais. I didn't know where I was at first. France, well that was a surprise. My aim was to get to England. I spoke good English, so surely I could get a job there? We were in a migrant camp for over six months. The cops wrecking it every so often. But at last, I booked a boat to England, it took every penny I had to get passage for the three of us. When I saw it, and how many there were, I didn't want to go. But they had guns, they shot a man in the foot, said the next one who complained they would kill. Too many, way too many, just pushed on board, utterly overcrowded. Impossible. All my money gone. I won't go in to detail of what happened. The dinghy too low in the water, choppy sea, the inevitable happened.' He stopped for a few seconds, eyes closed. 'My wife and son were drowned, and me almost, but saved by the lifeboat people and the NHS.'

He breathed deeply, overcome by memories.

'I am sorry to be asking these questions,' said Penny. 'Just say, if it is too much.'

He waved her on.

'Such memories are no stranger to me,' he said. 'Better to have them with friends and cake.'

Better not to have them at all, thought Jack, feeling uncomfortable at what the interview was bringing out.

'Why were you able to stay in the UK?' said Penny.

'I told the Home Office of my scientific papers. They didn't believe me, as I had no ID, all gone in the sea. A lady lawyer, who was working pro bono, such a lovely lady, Miriam, Jewish. I owe her so much. She was able to get in touch with Berkeley and they gave me a good reference. Even the Home Office accepted who I was. So, I could leave that transit camp, an awful place, like a prison, there were suicides, violence, all those traumatised people. But once I was free, it was tough. Rents are so high but I managed to get a job teaching at an FE college in Havering, below my expertise, but a job is a job. I was grateful for anything. I worked hard at it. No wife and child to distract me. So what else had I to do?'

He took a sip of tea.

'Have more cake, Penny, Jack. Please. I can't eat it all myself.'

Jack cut a slice for himself and Penny. Too sweet, but it was food and they'd had a long morning. Biscuits at Liz's. A sugary morning, his doctor would be shaking his head in dismay.

'They liked me at the college,' continued Deneb. 'I got good results in my classes. I was there two years, then I saw the advertisement for the job at Queen Mary University. I applied, and they took me on. Havering didn't want me to leave, but I had to go. Theoretical and particle physics is my field. And I had to get back into it before I became too out of date, the field moves on so quickly. I was so lucky to get a position. Again, Berkeley was my way in; my professor there gave me a good reference, that and my published papers.'

'I have seen you at Queen Mary's,' said Penny, 'but not often.'

'I don't socialise. I still have to make up for lost time. I am reading papers, updating my lectures. I stay out of the common room.'

'I understand,' she said. 'It is hard to keep up with all the new work coming in. Tempting as it is to go in the common room, you can waste a lot of time there. But if we can discuss yesterday's walk...'

'No problem. Please, ask what you need to.'

' At the snack break,' she said, 'when Mike went off to find the Witch's Tree, what did you see of the comings and goings?'

'Not so much,' said Deneb. 'I saw Phil go off, and heard a penny whistle playing, but I was reading a scientific paper on my phone. I needed it for Monday, for a lecture I was giving. I really shouldn't have been on the walk at all. But I needed to get out of the house. In the open air, I can breathe. Less bad memories.'

It was the way Jack felt about astronomy. His escape, not that he'd ever had to get out of a war zone and been on an overcrowded dinghy in the Channel. But in a small measure, he could understand.

'Who do you think might have killed Mike?' he said.

'I don't know. A girlfriend perhaps. He always had a new one on his arm. Like a new watch, he had to have someone. Or it could be someone connected with his business dealings. He was a hedge fund manager. I don't really know what that is, but I suspect he could be ruthless in business matters. No doubt he made enemies. But it wasn't me who killed him, should you be asking that. Why would I? He was just a walk leader as far as I was concerned. Not the nicest of people, but he led walks.' He shrugged. 'That's all I can tell you.'

Chapter 14

Once they'd left Deneb's, Penny drove off at once. He had been at the door seeing them off.

She said, 'I didn't want to chat outside his house. I'll stop in a minute or two.'

'The man's been through a lot,' he said.

'Difficult company though. I know I shouldn't say that, but he is so intense.'

'How dare I say that I am no good at small talk,' said Jack.

'You more than get by,' she said. 'Though not every woman is charmed by a lecture on the earth's magnetism.'

'You asked me what I'd been reading,' he insisted.

'It was a joke. It's like, 'how are you?' You are not expected to answer it literally.'

Jack blew out his cheeks. 'I shall go to an evening class on small talk. How to say nothing while eating cake.'

She stopped the car, took a deep breath and lay back.

'So what do we think of Deneb?' she said. 'Apart from his lack of small talk.'

'I thought he was a nice bloke. He's had a hard time. Lost his wife and child in the Channel, but he is making a life for himself.'

'I'd put him down for suicide, one day or another. Sorry. But it's that intensity. He's so alone.'

'At least he's part of the walking group.'

'People avoid him even there. He's too heavy. Too troubled.'

They didn't speak for a while. Jack thinking of unhappy people, made all the more unhappy, as the happy people avoid their company. The small talk society.

'Do you think he killed Mike?' she said.

'No,' he said. 'He's too unhappy to think that would help him.'

'He could be angry at Mike's showing off, his superficial lifestyle. Possessions maketh man.'

'They reveal his insecurity. Mike's, I mean. Buying showy stuff, so we'll know he's somebody.'

'Says a poor man.'

Jack half laughed.

'I can be a little jealous,' he said, 'but ten thousand pounds on a watch! That is so stupid.'

'Sounds like you would kill Mike.'

'I would just avoid him.'

'We are off piste again. Back to Deneb.'

'I can't imagine him killing Mike. There would have to be a far bigger motive than resentment at his showing off.'

'And his racism.'

He flicked a hand to brush her addition away. 'I don't see it.' Then stopped, reflecting. 'It's just possible, I suppose. A man on his own, so much on his own, could get very obsessive.'

'Not a total no then.'

'I want it to be no. But...' His intelligence battled with his feelings. 'I hope he didn't do it,' was all he could manage.

'I agree,' she said. 'But let's keep an open mind.'

An open mind put them all in the frame. Phil the boozer, Liz the West Ham fan, Deneb the sad. Nova, even. Penny, he couldn't rule out much as he wanted to. And Fiona, he hadn't said a word to her on the walk. He'd heard her argument with Phil, but could barely recall her face. Just in the circle at the beginning. A youngish black woman who has a cat called...'

'Who is Marcus Garvey?' he said.

'What is this about?'

'Fiona's cat.'

'Marcus Garvey. He was a fighter for black rights, a hundred years ago. A 'back to Africa' man. He thought whites would never give black people their rights. So he was into separatism. Black people had to be independent, and not be lackeys.'

'How do you know this?'

'Fiona told me. And now I must get home. Really. Two days have gone by. Yesterday on the walk, and now today interviewing. I've got lectures to prepare, a busy week ahead. I shall drop you off and then we must part. I have so much to do.'

She headed to Forest Gate.

'I've got to clear my head,' she said on the way. 'Think number theory, not murder, the uses of the square root of minus one, not who killed Mike Rayner.'

She stopped at Forest Gate police station. They embraced.

'Perhaps tomorrow evening, for an hour, no longer. I've too much on, as delightful company as you are, even when you are on about the earth's magnetism.'

And she left him to go in and give his statement.

Chapter 15

'How did it go?' said Mia looking up from her laptop at the sitting room table.

'We all killed him. Hand in glove, seven of us on the knife. One grand conspiracy.' He threw his jacket on the sofa. 'I am no wiser than when we started out. I'll make a cup of tea.'

'Have you had any lunch?'

'Cake and biscuits. What have we got that's easy to cook?'

'I made some lasagne,' she said.

'Without meat?' he said sceptically.

'I'll made lasagne,' she insisted, 'without a single dead animal.'

'What did you do for milk?'

'Oat milk, and before you ask, tofu for cheese.'

'Very healthy. I am sure it will save the planet. But I'd rather have a bacon sandwich.'

'You'll have to go and buy bacon then.'

Jack went into the kitchen. He had given his statement at the cop shop, for what it was worth. He hadn't been at his most attentive during the walk, spending too much time constructing a makeshift spoon from a yogurt lid. Hardly detective-level activities.

Feeling a little sickly after a morning of sugar, he went through the cupboards and fridge. Not a hint of meat, no cheese, no milk – real milk from real cows that is, not that pretend stuff from plants.

This is what happens when you have a vegan daughter, he thought. And don't shop yourself, he had to accept. There would be bacon if he had bought it. Ditto milk and cheese.

Dare he try the lasagne?

He opened the oven, the half-eaten dish was still warm. He sniffed at it. Not so bad, just it was against his religion; the meat eaters bible said this was abomination. Sin piled on sin.

Jack took a teaspoonful. Edible. It hadn't killed him. And he wouldn't have to cook.

He ladled some on a dish. Close your eyes and imagine it is meat. And he ate it. Not bad, not bad, just missing something. The tofu was somewhat bland, no bite to it. There was a fair bit of veg amongst the lentil. He'd spotted some celery, some carrots, peas. It would at least cancel the cake.

Jack had just finished eating when his phone rang.

Alison. His ex-wife. Mia's mother, his bane.

He awaited the customary earful.

'Hello, Alison,' he said, having some idea what this call would be about. Or rather whom it would be about.

'Hello, Jack,' she said. 'How are things going?'

'Fine.' He wasn't going to tell her about the murder, which would result in machine gun questioning for the next half-hour, and would be no help to him whatsoever.

'Is your daughter still adamant about leaving school?' she said.

He noted 'your daughter' but didn't take the bait.

'She tells me she has left. That you are unhappy about it, and that's why she's staying here for the time being.'

'And what do you think, Jack?'

'I'd rather she was at school.'

The kitchen door opened, and there was Mia listening in, to his half of the conversation.

'She's done all that work, Jack, and she's just going to throw it all away.'

'I'd rather she was at school,' he said, 'but I can't make her go. She's 17, 18 in a few months. She has to make her own mistakes.'

Mia showed thumbs up.

'All her teachers say she is very bright.'

'We know that,' said Jack.

'I really don't know what to do. We had a fearful row.'

'That's why she's here.'

'Tell her she can come home any time.'

'Your mother says you can come any time,' he called to Mia.

Mia shrugged.

'I won't waste any more of your time,' said Alison. But she would of course. 'I hate teenagers.'

They answer back, thought Jack.

'She's been working on my website,' he said to placate her. 'She's good at that sort of thing. I am going to see if I can get any work as a private investigator.'

'The Philip Marlowe of Forest Gate.'

'Don't sneer.'

'I am not sneering.'

'Kindle, don't quench.'

That was a favourite saying from Max, at Alcohol Halt, where he went from time to time when the need for alcohol gripped him.

'Who shall I kindle, you or her?' said Alison.

'It's not for me to say,' he said.

'I shan't stop her allowance.' No longer called pocket money. That was for kids, Mia had told them both.

'Sensible,' he said.

'She's not taking my calls, Jack.'

The upshot of a fearful row, he thought.

'I'll talk to her tonight,' he said. 'I'll tell her your thoughts, and we'll talk about what she intends doing with her life.'

Mia blew a raspberry and gave a thumbs down.

'Give her my love. Bye.'

Alison ended the call.

Mia came fully into the kitchen and sat on a chair.

'Don't tell me what she said. I know from your answers. I see you've eaten the lasagna.'

'It was better than cardboard.'

'You are rather ungrateful.'

'You're sounding like your mother.'

'Is she still saying the same thing?'

'Yes, but she wasn't shouting. And she's not stopping your allowance.'

'That's alright then. Make the tea, and I'll show you what I've done with your website.'

Chapter 16

Once made, they took the mugs of tea into the sitting room. At the table, she showed him on her laptop what she had done.

'How did you get me in a jacket and tie?'

'AI imaging. What do you think of the slogan?'

He read: *To Get it Back, Come to Jack.*

'To get what back?' he said.

'Whatever your client is looking for.'

'It's an awful lot to promise.'

'What do you want to say? To maybe get it back, come to Jack who will try to find it if he can.'

'More honest.'

They discussed the slogan for half an hour, as proper capitalists do. Then Jack vetoed it, as CEOs do. And Mia, miffed, went off to read a book in her bedroom.

How could he promise so much? This case, he wasn't even off first base. Jack laid back on the sofa and thought about the interviews they had done that day. He and Penny could come up with a motive for all three: Phil's resentment at not getting any more sales from Mike, Liz – a daughter abused by Mike, Deneb – getting back at racist Mike. All vague, maybe false. And he wasn't sure about Penny, who had been out with Mike, but then again, Mike did get around. Probably why he liked the walking group. Him as leader, looking over the potential.

Feeling somewhat abandoned, he phoned Penny. A short chat would hardly cut into her preparation.

She answered curtly. 'Yes?'

Jack wasn't prepared for that reaction, as if he were a cold caller selling insurance. There was a voice in the background, male, female, he couldn't be sure.

'I thought you might like to compare notes,' he said.

A long sigh. 'I am so busy, Jack.'

'Not so busy,' he said. 'Someone is with you.'

'A neighbour popped in for five minutes. Please don't start this possessive nonsense. We've only been out twice.'

Three times, he thought, but didn't say.

'Sorry to interrupt you,' he said. 'I'll leave you to your neighbour.'

'Are you always like this?'

'Like what?'

'Checking up. Jealous.'

'I just phoned to talk, a short chat, thinking we might swap thoughts on the interviews. I don't care about your neighbour. I don't want a row.'

'Neither do I, Jack. Goodbye.'

He stared at the phone screen as if it were to blame for the brutal halt. What had he done wrong? She had gone home to prepare for tomorrow, she had told him. And there she was talking to someone. Was that a sin? It could be a neighbour, a five minute chat. Though, is there such a thing? And she was so snappy. A short phone call and she was calling him jealous.

Jack felt like phoning back and yelling: he wasn't checking up, he wasn't jealous, and she could do what she damned well liked with her neighbour. None of which would have been wise. So he seethed. Was this another relationship down the tubes?

Getting off the sofa, and he marched about the sitting room, thrashing his arms, talking to her, telling her how reasonable he was being. How all he'd wanted to do was talk about the interviews. And she'd snapped at him like a hungry alligator. He trumped every reply she gave. In fact, she was rather weak, illogical. Her arguments simply didn't stack up.

Was she the killer?

Irritated as he was, he knew it wasn't at all reasonable to put her in the frame because he was bruised at her accusations. But that didn't mean she wasn't the killer.

He reflected how logic depended on mood. And discussed that with her. His mood, her mood. Who had the right to be angriest.

His phone rang.

Jack picked it up gingerly.

'Sorry,' she said.

'That's OK,' he said. 'I was a bit out of order.'

'No, no, I snapped at you.'

'Hardly snapped.'

'It was just my neighbour here.'

'Has he gone?'

'Don't start again.'

'I simply asked.'

'No you didn't. You implied that he is sitting here in silence, while I smooth over things with you. And then me and him get a laugh out of it, once I put the phone down.'

'That's a long train of surmise.'

'I don't like being asked my motives.'

'Did you kill Mike Rayner?'

Where that came from, he hardly knew, except it had been crawling around every thought about her, but never voiced, until this instant.

'Yes,' she said. 'During the snack break, I went to the Witch's Tree and stuck a knife in him. Vengeance is mine, I cried. And right now I am sharpening my blade, as you are about to be my next victim.'

'Do you kill all your boyfriends?'

'Most of them.'

They were quiet a while, he reflecting on what was being said, his anger and it seemed hers too. Though it didn't mean she wasn't the killer.

'I am sure you didn't kill him,' he said.

'I am not used to such praise.'

'Small talk isn't my best subject.'

'It has been noted.'

'We are getting very wrapped up. Emotional.'

'What do you think that means?'

'Conducting an affair around a murder is not to be recommended.'

'I shall put that in a Christmas cracker.'

'Sorry if I offended you, Penny. No, proper sorry. You can talk to your neighbour anytime you like, day or night.'

'I'm sorry too. Proper sorry. I was snappy. And you are right, you mostly are. It's been an emotional time. And suddenly, you strike out at the nearest person. Do you know, I have been walking up and down examining every word we said, hitting you like Punch bashing Judy. Smash, smash, smash. And it's all electricity, hormones, need. Words become weapons, knives, oh I shouldn't say knives. I didn't kill him, I retract my confession.'

'I accept it. And your apology. And thank you for phoning back.'

'I had to. I couldn't work like this. I was hoping you'd phone back first.'

'Sorry.'

'So you should be. But thank you for that. Now I must get to work. You know, you are not so bad at small talk. After all, what have we been saying?'

That we care about each other, he thought.

'A pile of words,' he said.

'Now I really must get back to work. Phone me tomorrow. When you do, I shall kick my neighbour out, and just speak to you. Bye.'

She ended the call. Jack lay back on the sofa. That was exhausting, like a frantic game of table tennis. But they had come together, called the game a draw, thrown their bats away and trodden on the ping-pong ball.

Jack went into his bedroom where Mia was flat out on the bed reading.

He said, '*To Get it Back, Come to Jack* – is a brilliant slogan.'

Chapter 17

Mia was in the sitting room working on Jack's website at the table. Peace reigned. Jack reflected on the row with Penny. They had both been so touchy. It took next to nothing to get them yelling at each other. But they had made up and the relief of it was sweet balm.

'Why are you smiling to yourself?' said Mia.

'Because my daughter has made a marvellous slogan that will have them queueing halfway down the street.'

'An exaggeration,' she said. 'But I'll take the compliment. I heard you shouting on the phone. Was that with Mum?'

'No, with Penny.'

'Didn't take long to get to that stage.'

'We have made up.'

'It won't last,' said the font of wisdom.

The doorbell rang.

Jack got up languidly, and went out of the flat. Going down the stairs, he endeavoured to stop smiling. Not so easy, he was feeling pleased with himself. He suspected his daughter was right. It wouldn't last.

He opened the front door.

Alison was there, in a green tracksuit, wearing no make-up, her long hair to her shoulders, still attractive, though not to him. Their marriage had wound itself well and truly out. She had a suitcase at her feet and a carrier bag.

'I'm not coming in,' she said. 'We'll only have a row. Not me and you. Me and Mia. I have brought her some clothes.' She indicated the suitcase. 'And some food for the two of you. Too much for me.' She lifted the carrier bag. 'It would only go off.'

'Any meat?'

'I've gone veggie, Jack. Your daughter's influence.'

'Thank you, anyway.'

She leaned towards him and said quietly, as if Mia was listening in, 'I am worried about her.'

'She's fine,' he said. 'Not on drugs, not slimming down to a stick, not emailing her network discussing how to end it all.'

'Could be worse,' she admitted. 'But I am a headteacher.' She laughed. 'Is that it really? Worried about my image. What people will think at my daughter leaving school without taking her exams.'

'I left school as soon as I could,' he said. 'With not a qualification in sight.'

'And here you are, sober as a judge and going to solve every crime in Forest Gate. Jack, you have decided me. I shall go in tomorrow and tell the kids, school is useless.'

He sang, *'Teachers, leave them kids alone!'*

'Pink stupid Floyd,' she exclaimed. 'Millionaire rock band telling kids that school is a waste of their time.'

'It's just another brick in the wall!'

'It's tosh, absolute codswallop. And you know it.'

'I do,' he said. 'I feel my ignorance every day.'

She looked at him quizzically, unsure whether he was teasing.

'You're better than you were. Why ever did I marry such a dumb cluck?'

'You tell me.'

'I saw potential. How wrong can a girl be!'

'Kindle, don't quench,' he said.

'Oh, that's a good tag, can I use it?'

'Only if you apologise for your past abuse.'

'That would take ages.' She kissed him on the cheek. 'Must go, Jack. Kindle, don't quench. I shall try that in assembly instead of education is useless.'

And she was off down the path.

Chapter 18

Jack was at the shop eight o'clock prompt. Mrs Elks was waiting for him. She had given him the keys, so he could open up and close up himself, but she was always there first thing. Impatient, often with additions for the work.

Mrs Elks was middle-aged, always in long, colourful dresses. He adjudged she wanted to stand out, be a presence. He had quite fancied her to begin with. That didn't last long, once they got down to business. She had a slight accent, being from Holland. They had begun on friendly terms, chatting about non-work matters, she had two daughters almost grown up, and he had one. Something in common. Her husband was an accountant, which perhaps was the reason she was so tight on costs. Or was she living beyond her means? She certainly wasn't going to tell him, though it mattered, as he needed to get paid, no matter her financial situation.

She lived on Windsor Road, not far away, walking distance, which was why she could always be here first thing. Coming to her house for the first time, she had asked him to take off his boots before entering. He had a hole in his sock, but then he hadn't anticipated having to take his boots off. Mrs Elks wasn't happy with the state of his overalls, especially when he sat on her pristine sofa with its cushions and throws. She had the tidiest house he had ever come across, one designed for discomfort. After just one more visit, they met henceforth at the shop where the work was being done. Better for both their states of mind. They no longer discussed the personal, just the work.

Jack was fitting out what was to be a curtain shop. He had been at it for two weeks, having, so far, plastered the walls, repaired floorboards, windows and the front door. Now it was the shop furniture: counters, shelves, rails and cupboards. Today, he'd be starting on the counters.

Mrs Elks was looking about the shop, with a frown that seemed to Jack to have become a permanent fixture. Though perhaps she just wore it for tradespeople. Jack had to be dogged with her, she was sharp, always wanting additions for the same price. He had constantly to refer her back to the agreement that she and he had signed. In his early days as a builder, word of mouth had been sufficient, except when it proved not to be, as who said what could be argued until the cows came home. Now, any job, beyond fixing a stuck window, had an agreement signed in blood, which he could always bring out from his back pocket. It didn't stop arguments, but he had a second in his corner.

'I am not happy about the office,' she said.

She was referring to the back room. They had agreed that Jack could use it as his office as a consulting detective, which he sometimes called himself, or private investigator, or just detective, depending on who he was talking to. Not that he'd had a single paying job yet as detective, but he had cards, a website, and an office at the back of a curtain shop.

'I agreed to give you 50% off the work,' he said, 'in lieu of rent for the back office for a year.'

She shook her head. 'It isn't feasible.'

'But you agreed.' He pulled out the agreement from his backpack, much fingered from being pulled out on previous occasions. 'It's here, signed by both of us.'

Though he had never been sure about the back office. Not here. Not with Mrs Elks patrolling the shop like a frontier guard once the shop opened, and pointing out the deficiencies in his work as soon as he entered each day.

'If you want, we can make a new agreement,' he said, 'you can pay the full price and I will forego the office.'

'I will need the office,' she insisted. 'I should never have made the agreement. You caught me at a weak moment.'

'We can make a new agreement,' he repeated.

She strolled about looking at plastering and floorboards. Impossible to tell if she was satisfied or not. Perhaps he should sweep up more, satisfy Mrs Elks' cleanliness gene, which Alison had told him he lacked. He tried in work-spaces. In the shop, he always did a clean up at the end of the day, but never spruce enough to eat your dinner off, as his employer probably wanted.

'I shall talk to my husband,' she said.

He was already working out what new agreement they could come to. A detective office here would never work. Not with her territorial imperative at the front. She would terrify any of his customers. Then again, she would have her shop workers to criticise, be the bane of their lives instead of his. Mrs Elks had another curtain shop in Ilford. Jack had gone there with her at the beginning to get the feel of what she wanted. He could see at once, the shop workers were intimidated by her, a man and two young women, all Asians. He had gone there once without her, and they'd all agreed, along with him, that she was a tyrant. And no doubt would die filthy rich with a trail of misery in her wake.

Or go bankrupt by overreaching herself.

He was prepared to give her a 15% discount, instead of the 50%, and give up the office. But he wasn't going to tell her that. As soon as he'd mention any figure, she would beat him down. Thank heavens he had the agreement, the testament that both had signed.

She said, 'Why do you want the office?'

'For my detective agency,' he said.

Sometimes, he believed in the agency, but not now, in her demonstration of tough business practices. This is how you had to be to make money. Be hard as nails and take no prisoners.

'It won't work,' she said. 'No one round here wants a private detective.'

That could very well be true, but it was no good admitting any weakness to Mrs Elks.

'We have done our market research,' he said.

A lie, an utter, barefaced lie. He and Mia were going to put out some ads, along with the website, and hope that enough people in the area wanted a private detective. By doing it.

'What do you charge?' she said.

'It depends on the job,' he said. He and Mia had some tentative figures in mind, but they had never been tested in the storm of the market.

Fortunately, Mrs Elks knew less about private detectives than he did. So she didn't press him for actual figures. Though he could have given her some. So much an hour, so much a day. All surmise, fictions, who knew whether they would ever be facts?

'I have seen businesses come and go,' she said. 'This is a bad time for the high street.'

So why are you setting up a shop on the high street, he might have said. But didn't. Though it told him things were tight. Perhaps the Ilford shop wasn't doing too well. But his knowledge of curtain shops matched hers on detective agencies.

Over the weekend, Jack should have made up an invoice for the work done so far, but the walk with Penny and her crowd and the aftermath, then the interviews yesterday, what with his daughter arriving, had squeezed his time away like toothpaste in a tube. He must make an interim invoice this evening.

Finally, Mrs Elks left.

Jack sighed with relief. The space was his. He could do some work without the stress of her around. Customers! The work was fine, mostly, but you never knew with customers. They might start off charming but they could soon change. He had had all sorts. Some he'd almost loved, others he couldn't wait to get away from, with the rows over work and fights for payment.

The shop was 15 yards long and 10 wide with a large front window with pull down external shutters. It had been a dress shop, and then a luggage shop, in the tale of failures along Woodgrange High Street. The certainties were fast food, bookies, greengrocers and supermarkets. Anything else fought the dragons of the internet. The Pound Shop was no longer a pound shop at all. Inflation killed that incarnation. Now a two or three Pound Shop.

Jack looked at what he'd done so far. She had no right to complain. He'd done a good job plastering the walls. It was almost like a dance, slapping the plaster on before it dried. Quite a knack to it. You had to lay out cover sheets, but with the plaster at the right consistency, and the right amount on the board, slapped and smoothed down quickly, you minimised drips. Just don't stop, keep it going.

Today he would work on the counters, two were to be made. Each would have a flat top to lay curtains along, drawers in the back and a flat front, which would be curtained, though that was beyond his shop fitting, and in her decorous hands. The first step was frames for the counters, hopefully finishing them before the day was done. Unless he got snowed under with detective work.

Ho, Ho. Fat chance.

The wood for the frame lay in a bundle, delivered on Friday. The longest ones had been cut to size, the shorter uprights and side lengths he must saw to size.

Jack was marking up, when Mia arrived. She had her backpack with her laptop in and whatever, as it was quite full. She would work in the back office while he worked out here, they'd agreed last night. She'd work on the website and put out on social media that Forest Gate Investigations was open for business.

The office had a battered desk and two chairs, left by the last occupant, who by the number of bills coming for them, had most likely gone bankrupt. Jack and Mia had bought a kettle and four cups with floral patterns that Mia had bought from the Pound Shop. The additional cups were for clients. Not customers, Mia had insisted.

'Customers make it sound like a shop,' she'd said.

'Clients make it sound like a dentist,' Jack had replied.

He continued marking up with pencil, set square and steel tape. He was getting quite slick at it.

'Has the moose been in?' asked Mia, who'd had to face Mrs Elks a couple of times.

'It can't work,' he said. 'Not here, with her out here, we in the back office. I would dread coming in every morning.' He put the pencil behind his ear. 'It was never a good idea, an office, here, behind a shop.'

'Sorry,' said Mia. 'I talked you into it.'

'I didn't have to agree.' Jack walked up to the front window, and looked out to the rush hour high street, as if that might help. All those people walking by, how many needing a private investigator? Anyone's guess. He turned about. 'How do we get out of it?'

Mia thought for a few moments, then said: 'We must make it that she doesn't want us here.'

'She doesn't want us,' said Jack. 'She wants the office herself.'

Mia looked at him puzzled. 'So what's the problem?'

'The discount,' said Jack. 'We have given her 50% off. If we just walk out, then she gets the work for half price. And I'm working at a loss.' He looked at the shop space, the door of the office, their office for the time being, and shook his head. 'We just may have to do it. It was a dumb deal.'

'Suppose she really wants us out?' said Mia.

'She does.'

'No, I mean even more than we want to go.'

Jack thought on this. How could they make life unpleasant for her. Make *her* dread coming in.

'Got any ideas?'

'One or two,' she said cryptically. 'Tomorrow, we fight back.'

Jack laughed. She had cheered him up. It was good having the company, even if she should be at school. But one thing at a time. Leave it to his eco-warrior to sort out the hassle of the office.

'I'll make us tea,' said Mia. 'I've made some sandwiches.' She patted her backpack. 'Peanut butter.'

He might have said, that's for kids, but there was no point starting a vegan versus carnivore argument. He needed her on his side. Besides which, he was peckish, having only had toast and tea, in order to get here at 8 am, so the moose had no complaints. He had picked up Mia's derogatory nickname for their employer, or as Mia put it, nom-de-guerre.

From what he could fathom, Mia was out to give the moose a string of complaints.

Mia went into the back room.

'Wait a sec!' he called into the office where Mia was getting out her laptop and sandwiches.

'Detective work,' he said.

'Do we get paid?'

'Just practice.' She blew a raspberry, he ignored it. 'Professor Penny Hicks, mathematics department of Queen Mary's University. Can you find out who her last husband was? And his contact details.'

'Do you always do this for your dates?'

'Only if murder is involved.'

'You want me to find his gravestone,' she said.

'I sincerely hope not.' That would kill any romance and maybe himself. 'I'd like to talk to him, that's all. Find out about her. The investigation. Go to it.'

'Yes, squire.'

He left and returned to marking up the uprights, working on the floor. It was automatic work once you knew the measurements. Important, as you didn't want to waste wood, which was growing more expensive by the day. The counters had to look good. Not just to satisfy his fussy employer but himself too.

He thought of Penny, as he went through the lengths of wood, rapidly marking them up. Last night had been pleasant. That is after the row, the making up. So now he was investigating her husband. If she ever found out... One step at a time. Mia had come up with nothing yet.

Though she'd hardly got going.

Last night, think about such pleasant things, the row had been needed in order to make up afterwards. It did add stress to a relationship. You never knew quite where you were. Penny had been married. Twice, did she say? If so, she wasn't that good at finding life partners. With each, she would have been in love to begin with, always an elastic element comprising everything and nothing, but the romance, whatever it had been, had drained away like dirty water, in the routines of cooking, cleaning, sharing or not sharing.

A chat with her last husband might not reveal anything beyond resentment. Or might reveal a side of her he had not seen. Innocuous or carnal.

Did he mean carnal? A more evil side revealed in her marriage, anyway.

Alison had complained, in his one and only marriage, that he never did the washing. And when he did, so it had never been never, hung the washing out so badly, she'd had to re-peg it. But by that time, she was finding fault with everything he did.

Don't mar a new relationship when it has barely begun, he reminded himself. Talking to her husband was just insurance. He needed to know whether she was a killer or not. Likely, it would come to nothing. Besides, he might not do it, because if she ever found out that he was checking up on her, that would kill their relationship, sure as eggs were for throwing at lying politicians.

The making up with her had been reassuring, soothing, hopeful. And over the phone too. They had both wanted to apologise, to say, without actually saying it, that they cared for each other. He didn't want to find any skeletons in her cupboard. Should he call Mia off? What do you even say to her ex, her last ex? Mia had told him how to behave to clients. You give them a card, and act like a professional.

Not like a nervous lover.

What was the best time to phone Penny? She'd be busy with students, with her mathematical colleagues, and other professorial stuff. Imagine phoning a professor. But she hadn't been one last night, not on the phone.

Had she killed Mike Rayner?

The worm in the apple. The fact that he cared for her didn't answer the question. And asking her, point blank, like he did yesterday, was stupid. There was only one answer she would give him, whether guilty or innocent.

Penny had confidence and she had had a relationship with Mike. Insufficient data, as she had said about something else, but it didn't stop him mulling over the insufficiency, as if there might be something there that he had missed.

Either he should talk to her ex-husband, or leave things as they are, and let their relationship develop.

The front door of the shop opened and in came Nova along with the traffic noise of the high street. She shut the door.

'Good morning, Jack.'

'Good morning, Nova.'

Here was a surprise.

She was obviously working today, smartly outfitted as Detective Constable Nova Taylor. In plain clothes, but she was Detective Inspector Fayyad Kamani's sidekick, and he insisted on the importance of appearance.

Nova wore a navy blue dress suit, a white blouse, her blonde hair neatly tied back in a ponytail, and was shod in brown flats. Never heels of any sort, though she was quite short. You can't run in heels, she had told him. Save them for parties.

'You don't look like a detective,' she said, looking over Jack in his overalls.

He laughed. 'I can't match you. But there's detectives and detectives. And I'm the latter.'

She smiled, then said, 'I've something to confess. About Saturday's walk.'

He thought back to Saturday, ages ago now, when he'd met the others at Forest Gate station. And it hit him, all at once. Why had he never thought it before? Of course. It had to be. Nova and Mike were hardly on the same page.

'You were undercover,' he said.

'I wondered if you'd work it out.'

'Not until now. But Saturday, at the railway station, soon as you saw me, you took me aside and said, don't tell anyone I'm a cop. And clearly you didn't like me being on the walk.'

'There was me telling everyone I work for the Council, and along comes this bloke who knows that's a lie.'

'It was hard to believe that you and Mike were an item. But then...' He shrugged. 'I suppose he had his charms for some.'

'Professional,' she said. 'Purely professional. It was believed Mike was trading in stolen paintings. And I volunteered to go undercover to get evidence. That was some job. I had to learn about art, a crash course. For a week, I had a one to one tutor, can you believe. She took me to the Tate Gallery, Tate Modern, the National Gallery.' She enumerated on her fingers. 'I learnt about the Impressionists, the Pre-Raphaelites, about DaVinci, Michelangelo, Modigliani, Picasso, Rodin, Epstein, Turner, Constable. And then some moderns, like Tracy Emin, Damien Hirst, and who's that woman did those eye confusing black and whites in the 60s...' She struggled. 'Oh, what's her name. See, in one ear and out the other.'

'No idea,' said Jack. 'My ex-missus used to drag around galleries, trying to give me some culture.'

'You never will be Renaissance Man, Jack.' She snapped her fingers. 'Bridget Riley, Op Art, really eye boggling stuff.' She smirked, pleased at having got there. 'But anyway, I had to know enough to impress Mike. I was given a pile of books to take home, postcards galore. I was bunged to the gunnels with art. But it worked. I joined the walking group, went on a walk that Mike was leading. I told him, at one point, that the sky was like a Constable painting, and so we talked about Constable's realism and about Turner as the first impressionist. The upshot was he invited me to a private view in a Mayfair gallery.'

'Did you sleep with him?'

She smiled at the question, as if expecting it.

'No, I didn't. I wouldn't. Dates were fine, galleries and museums, of course. He took me back to his place a couple of times, showed me his art collection, tried it on, and I made it plain that bed wasn't on the cards.'

Jack could imagine how she had made it plain. Nova might be short, but was an expert in martial arts to make up for her stature.

'Mike loved it that I was OK with him dating others,' she went on. 'He could bed them, fine by me, but I was his art chic.' She screwed up her nose. 'That was his term, not mine, sexist pig. But I wasn't going out with him to challenge his patronising views on women. Art bonded us. What a fraud I was. We'd talk about the influence of African masks on Picasso, as if I hadn't just read it up the night before.' She wiped her brow at the remembered effort. 'It was one hell of a stretch. I was reading up half the night, making sure I'd got things right that day and then preparing for the exhibition we were going to.' She laughed at a memory. 'I got very good at saying *I agree, Mike*. My cover story was the history of art degree I did at Newcastle University. I went up there for a day. I talked to a tutor, so I'd know something about the course. But Mike bought it. I had become arty enough to take him in.'

'Did you find out what he was up to?'

He had stopped working, intrigued by Nova's deception. Pleased that she hadn't been enthralled by Mike, and wondering why she was here, telling him this. Surely not just to fill him in on her undercover role on the walk.

'Mike had a special side room. He kept it locked, but he let me see what was in there. A veritable treasure trove that he kept on the move, buying and selling on. And some of those were acquired dubiously. I was wired with a camera and mic. Mike was going to be arrested any day, when, as you well know, he beat the rap, as you might say.'

'By the Witch's Tree.'

They were silent a while. She was looking around at the shop, at what he was doing. But he knew she wasn't really looking.

'Why are you telling me this?' he said. 'Fascinating as it is.'

'I'm off the case,' she said with a shrug. 'Too involved. I was undercover, but a suspect to those not in the know. The accused's solicitor would object to me being on the investigation team. So there we are, I'm off the case. Let others find the murderer. My presence is not required.' She hesitated before going on. 'Please keep mum that I was undercover. At least, for now.'

'You didn't answer my question.'

After a pause, while she looked him square in the eye, she said, 'I wondered, how me and you are.'

He wondered too.

'You have been going out with Penny?' she said.

'We've had a few dates,' he admitted, carefully. 'It's reached the maybe stage.'

'Well if it gets to maybe not, I am still here.'

They were a couple of yards apart in the work space, the builder and the now arty cop. His feelings for her hadn't quite died. Like glowing embers, they were flaming with her breath.

'I could take you to the Tate Gallery,' she said.

Neither moved. Not quite knowing the score. The maybe, the maybe not. They had been lovers, they had quarrelled, agreed to have a break, which was often the end of the affair.

'I'd prefer Wanstead Flats,' he said.

'Why not both? We have time enough. It would be such a waste me knowing all this art, and not sharing it with someone who is not a crook.'

He could imagine them arm in arm walking through a gallery and she pointing out what he was looking at. That's a thingmebob, that's by whatshisface and indicating what he should be seeing. Ignorance is not bliss, not at all. Not taking any exams at school had been the foolhardiness of youth. He could learn, with the right teacher.

'How about tonight?' she said. 'The Flats. The Orionids are active.'

She was referring to a meteor shower which came around in autumn. It was a temptation. With the right teacher.

'Mars is well positioned too.'

Very tempting.

'You know how to say such sexy things,' he said.

Her phone rang.

She answered it impatiently.

'Yes, sir. I'll be right along.'

Swiftly, she stepped across to Jack, and kissed him on the cheek. A rapid dusting and then drew back.

'I'll be at your place at eight. Bring a thermos as well as your telescope. Must rush. The boss wants me at the station an hour ago.'

And she was out the door.

Chapter 19

Jack worked on through the morning. Finishing the marking up, he set up his electric saw on his workbench and cut the pieces that would make up the counter frames. The saw screeched, sawdust flew, hitting his goggles, while he dwelt on Nova's visit. Her role on the walk, coming here to tell him what she had really been doing. All hush hush. And setting up a date on the Flats. He laughed at that, as the saw raced greedily through the wood. Who else would be so tempted to go out on a cold autumn night? Two stargazers out in the gloom to watch the Orionid shooting stars, and hoping for a view of Mars. Who else?

Could be muddy. Best bring his big thermos.

All the pieces sawn, he put them into two piles, either side of the shop, one lot for each counter. He'd assemble them after lunch.

What had she said as she left?

'I'm still here.'

Was he? Recalling why he and Nova had cooled off. She was so tied up when on a case. With no time for anything else. That was bearable, but when she did find time, too often the date was cancelled. Work took precedence over everything else. 'I am a detective,' she would declare as if that excused leaving him waiting outside a cinema or alone in a restaurant.

Maybe, when all the clients came (with Mia's brilliant website), he would say the same thing to her. 'I am a detective!' Fat chance. And not here, never here, under the hawk-like gaze of Mrs Elks. That had to be sorted out.

108

Mia came out of the office, her hair awry, as if she had been running her fingers through it. He'd like to tell her to brush it, but they had discussed such things. She was a junior partner, and should be treated as such, here anyway. Not that he was a 'tidy your room' parent. He couldn't be, as his natural inclination was untidiness, unless it was at a client's place or he had a visitor.

She said, 'I found him.'

'Who?'

'Penny's husband. Ex, I mean. George Taplow. I have an email address too.'

'How did you find him?'

She shrugged. 'Easy enough. I Googled all the variations of Professor Penny Hicks, her college, her mathematics. There's quite a lot on her. Then I came up with wedding photos, about five years old, so I chased up the groom.' She beamed. 'Quite good fun actually.'

Mia gave him a scrap of paper on which she had scrawled the name and email of Penny's ex. Just about legible.

'Good work, Robin.'

'I'm not impressed with the Bat Cave,' she said indicating the coating of sawdust on the floor. 'And as for the Bat Mobile...'

They both laughed at the thought of his old van. Hardly the glamorous wheels of knight errant crime fighters.

'Let me have your cash card,' said Mia, 'and I'll pop up to the Co-op and buy us some lunch.'

He handed over his card. 'No more than a tenner.'

She took it, saying, 'Of course, Alfred should be doing this.'

'Who?'

She rolled her eyes in mock exasperation. 'Bruce Wayne's butler, of course. Too much time at the telescope and going out for walks with your latest squeeze, if you ask me.'

And left the shop.

He grinned as she strolled away. Good to have some company on the job. And maybe he should go and see a movie or two. The question was, who with? He brushed that aside, looking again at the scrap of paper. What should he do about George Taplow, Penny's ex-husband, the latter of two? He could do nothing. Probably the sensible course. The other, contact him, in order to question him about Penny.

What would a real detective do?

Jack went into the office. A detective now, he'd left the builder in the shop with the tools and sawdust, and tapped out an email on his phone, saying, very politely, that he'd like to talk to Mr Taplow about his ex-wife, and signing off, as Jack Bell, Private Investigator.

It was the last two words that halted him from sending. They seemed one hell of a cheek, putting himself in the same league as Sherlock Holmes, Poirot, and Philip Marlowe on the mean streets of LA. Here was Jack Bell in his builder's overalls, on the mean streets of Forest Gate, hesitating about sending off his first missive as PI. Would it impress, or would it be deleted as spam?

Private Investigator!

He weighed it up. You have to have some cheek, or everything is too much to take on. You must be willing to go into unwelcoming rooms. It was all very daunting. So much easier sawing wood, but then again, he had the Mrs Elks of the world to deal with and one had to stand one's ground, or be pushed aside.

The private investigator pressed send. Then went into the shop, instant transition to builder, and swept up the sawdust.

Chapter 20

Jack made the tea to go with the sandwiches and fruit that Mia had bought. Left to himself, he'd have gone to the greasy spoon up the road and had the works with chips, sausages, and multifarious ultra-processed food stuffed with cholesterol, fat, sugar, salt, colouring, flavour enhancers and who knows what else. Tasty, slow poisons, habit-forming chemicals, designed to keep addicts munching to keep their appointment with a heart attack.

'Got enough to do this afternoon?' he asked Mia, as they were tidying up after lunch in the office.

Mia nodded. 'Plenty. There's the website, and other outlets to put us on the map. And some eco folks I have to contact.'

Jack left her to it, leaving the office, her domain, and went out into the shop, his. Crossing the boundary brought Mrs Elks to mind. His customers/clients (whichever) would have to cross her territory and probably have to ask her where Forest Gate Investigations were. It would be on the office door, but how visible with her rails and paraphernalia?

No, he must get out of here. Work from home, or find somewhere else that wasn't a war zone.

Jack began assembling the frame for the counters, in the busyness of work pushing Mrs Elks out of his head. All the pieces of wood for the two frames had been cut to size. He grouped the long pieces, the legs, and side pieces. He was using metal Ls for the joints. Strong enough, and they would all be covered with board. The electric screwdriver buzzed, all but glowing in its rage, as the screws whirled into place.

He enjoyed this element of the work, all the sawn pieces coming together for the frame of a counter, making sense of his earlier work, and showing his calculations were correct. The logic of it appealed. Jack had to concentrate on the work in hand, aware he hadn't been thinking about the moose for all of quarter of an hour. Or Penny, or Nova. His head his own for this little while.

Not that the work was difficult, straightforward carpentry, but you needed to know what you were doing, where you were going and have everything to hand.

He had a rickety counter, with cross pieces still to go in place, when his phone rang.

Penny. Best take care. He put down his power screwdriver.

'Hello, Penny,' he said.

'I'm between classes and meetings,' she said. 'Just time for a quick chat. I managed to get to the cop shop yesterday, for my statement. So all legal and kosher; no one going to burst into my lecture with a warrant. What are you up to?'

'I'm in the shop I told you about, in the middle of making the frames for a couple of counters.'

'No detective work then?'

He certainly was not going to tell her about having found her ex. And having emailed him for a meeting.

'No, I'm shopfitting. Sawing, drilling, and putting in hundreds of screws. This is going to be a curtain shop. And I would really enjoy it if it wasn't for the tartar who is my employer.'

Normally, he would not criticise customers (or clients, he called them both interchangeably) with other people, as it might get back to them. But he didn't want to talk about detective work, not when she was the subject of his investigation. In fact, there was quite a lot he couldn't talk to her about, but shop work was fine. He could have taken her through every saw cut and screw fitting.

She said, 'I've classes and meetings until quite late. I was thinking, I could pop over to your place about eightish.'

Alarm bells rang. Someone was due at that very time.

'I'm busy,' he said quickly. 'Bookkeeping, invoices, you know how it is?'

'All vital,' she said. 'But I am sure you can put them aside for half an hour. I'll pop into Marks and get a cake. Must go. See you tonight.'

He might just have been able to interrupt her if he'd had his story straight. Bookkeeping was a useless excuse, as of course it can be laid aside. He should have said, I'm seeing a customer, giving them an estimate, their place. A big job. Don't know when I'll be back. But he hadn't. The best he could do was make sure he was out when she came. Be well over the Flats, and give Mia some tale to send her away. The customer one, it had just come in. That would do.

Two lies for Penny. Not good. One on her ex. Well, not really a lie, an omission. Though he was just trying to exonerate her from an accusation of murder. A pretty feeble line. Yes, he was, but he couldn't get it out of his head that she could be the actual killer. That's why he wanted to talk to her ex. Find out, from someone who knew her for years, what she was really like.

And the second lie. He didn't want to say he was going out with Nova tonight. So all that twaddle about invoices and books... Sure, he had some to do, but today or tomorrow wasn't imperative. Quite simply, he wanted to keep his options open. He wasn't sure about Nova, nor about Penny, and so wanted to keep two balls in the air until one got too weighty to catch.

Penny could be a murderer.

Nova could be all the hassle she was before.

Jack went back to putting in screws. Therapy for a two-timing builder.

He had just completed the first counter frame, when Deneb and Phil came into the shop.

Chapter 21

The pair were dripping wet. While Jack had been working, he'd been oblivious of the rain, pouring down the shop window, rivulets coalescing at the bottom.

The two of them were dressed almost the way they had been on the walk. Phil's wet, bald dome glistened in the strip light, with even less colour in his pale red jacket. Deneb had the addition of a peaked cap and black trainers, while Phil still wore his muddy boots.

Phil shut the rain out.

'It's coming down in buckets,' he exclaimed. He took his wringing jacket off, and finding nowhere for it, lay it on the floor.

'Hang on a sec,' said Jack.

He went into the office. Mia had on headphones, and was deep into something on her laptop as he took the other two chairs into the shop.

'Please,' said Jack, indicating one each.

Deneb took off his anorak, and put it on the back of the chair, revealing a white shirt and a pale blue tie. His trainers were wet, and no doubt his socks but he had no wish to take them off, suffering the discomfort of wet feet. Phil was fine with his boots, but his wet trousers would have to dry on him.

'We have been to the police station,' said Deneb.

'Third interview I have given the fuzz,' said Phil. 'Third! My pee in the forest is somehow suspicious.' He laughed. 'I don't think they know what they are doing. Lousy tea they make. No biscuits.'

'We met there,' said Deneb. 'And then the rain came down, so suddenly.'

Jack put his head into the office. He mimed to his headphoned daughter, and mouthed tea, showing three fingers, before returning to his guests.

'How did you know I was here?' he said.

'I saw it on the internet,' said Deneb. 'Jack Bell, Forest Gate Investigations. And this address. I wanted to talk to you, so it was lucky it was near the police station.'

'A lifesaver in a storm,' said Phil, trying to look out of the window though the drippy murk. 'Forest Gate Investigations eh? So do you know who the killer is?' He chuckled. 'It's like one of these murder mystery weekends the club set up a few years ago. We all had a role. I got killed. Great fun. Except this one is real.' He clapped his hands. 'Makes it all the more exciting.'

'I don't find it exciting at all,' said Deneb. He had sat down on one of the chairs, attempting to wipe moisture out of his chilly trouser legs.

'There's seven of us,'went on Phil. 'Us three, Liz the West Ham supporter, never trust them, I'm Arsenal, always have been, Penny the prof, Fiona the black lives matter more-than-any-others lady, and Nova the cop. The lying cop. She told us she worked for the Council, in the accounts office. What was that all about?'

Jack knew, but wasn't at liberty to say.

'Cops don't want to tell everyone they are cops,' said Deneb. 'I understand that.'

'But she soon took charge,' came in Phil. 'The moment we found Mike, she was bossing us about like a primary school teacher.'

'That's cops for you,' said Jack. 'She had to keep the crime scene clean.'

'You would know, Mr Private Investigator. Can you believe it, just eight of us. including Mike, and we have a cop and a private eye among them.' He peered at Jack, sucking his lower lip. 'Who were you investigating?'

'Client confidentiality,' he said without thinking of the implications.

That took Phil aback.

'You mean someone was employing you?' Jack nodded. Too late to back out of his lie. 'One of us on the walk?'

'Client confidentiality,' he repeated. His was a detective agency without clients, and here he was making one up.

'You came with Penny,' he said. 'Bet it was her.'

'Could be Mike,' said Deneb.

'Someone during the snack break,' said Jack trying to get them off him, 'one of us, went off and did it.' He paused, then added, 'You went off, Phil.'

'To pee or not to pee, that is the question.' He laughed at his own wit. 'I didn't kill anyone. Why would I? A call of nature. You can't deny me that. Can you?'

Mia came out of the office with a tray of three teas. There were sachets of sugar on a plate that she had been collecting from coffee shops for the past couple of weeks, since she'd known they were going to set up the agency.

She put the tray on the floor.

'Help yourselves,' she said. 'Sorry, no biscuits.'

And went back to the office.

'My daughter,' said Jack.

'The only non suspect on the premises,' said Phil. 'Except I don't suspect myself. So that leaves six of you. I don't exempt cops or private eyes. Both can kill.' He turned to Deneb. 'And physicists too.'

'*Now I am become Death, the destroyer of worlds,*' said Deneb.

When Phil looked at him in puzzlement, he added:

'Robert Oppenheimer said that. He was in charge of the construction of the atom bomb at Los Alamos during the Second World War. A theoretical physicist who I can identify with. The quote is from the Bhagavad Gita, a Hindu holy book.'

'There we are then. A precedent. And what a big one.'

'But artists don't have clean hands,' said Deneb. 'Caravaggio was a killer, was he not?'

'Indeed, indeed,' said Phil as he sipped his tea. Dissatisfied, he sprinkled in several sugar sachets. 'And some of Tracy Emin's work is criminal.' He chortled. 'And don't get me on the critics. They should all be put against the wall and shot.'

'Would you do the shooting?' said Jack.

Phil smirked. 'After the revolution,' he said.

'O'Brien would have approved, I am sure,' said Deneb. Seeing Phil nonplussed, he added, '1984, Room 101, rats.'

'Ah yes!' said Phil, taking a long draught of tea. 'The rats, the rats, crawling over his head. *Do it to Julia*, he cries.' Phil laughed. '*Do it to Julia!*' He turned to the others. 'What torture would it take for anyone of us to make such a betrayal?'

No one spoke. Jack shuddered. Torture could make you say anything, betray anyone.

Attempting to shake off the hell of Room 101, he said, 'You sold a painting to Mike.'

'I did. I did. Got well paid too,' he said smugly.

'Just one painting,' said Jack. 'Why no others?'

Phil shrugged uncomfortably.

'One is better than none,' he said.

Jack wondered whether it was, as with one you hope for more.

'You must have tried to sell him others,' said Jack.

'Wouldn't you?' exclaimed Phil. 'He had pots of money. Didn't know what to do with it all. Ten thousand pound watches. One of those, and he could have had 10 of my paintings. No, twenty. A job lot.' He stood up and put his coat on. 'He could be mean, tight fisted.'

'Would you stand him against the wall?'

'If I was Stalin...' He chuckled. 'Lucky for the world, I am not.' He looked at the two of them, their dismayed faces. 'Joking, joking. Don't you understand black humour?'

'It easily becomes bad taste,' said Deneb. 'Thou shalt not kill.'

Phil harrumphed. 'Too preachy for me, mate. I'm off to the pub. The Forest Tavern.' He peered through the shop window at the weather. 'The rain has almost stopped. I'll dry off in the pub anyway. What could be more welcoming?' He headed for the door. 'Thanks for the tea.'

And was out the door.

Chapter 22

When the shop door had closed on him, Jack said, 'What do you make of Phil?'

Deneb said, 'I know his sort. Too well. Your friend, your good neighbour, until the fascists take over. And then he'll hand you over for thirty pieces of silver. For your house, for your land.'

'That's a heavy judgement,' said Jack.

'I am a man of peace,' said Deneb. 'I've seen too much war. And what it can do to ordinary people, hand them a gun, a stripe on their shoulder and a flag to salute, and neighbours can be shot like game birds.'

Too much for Jack, trying to imagine himself in a civil war, though he suspected Phil could swing in any direction that favoured himself. But then how was he, himself, so different? War singles out the brave and the cowards.

Which was he?

He should get back to work, and leave philosophy to the professors. But he suspected Deneb was staying for a reason, and not just to keep dry.

'You can take your shoes off,' he said, looking at his wet trainers.

'I am not sure...' Deneb began.

'None of us are followers of fashion here.'

Deneb smiled and took off his shoes. His black socks were sodden.

'I stepped into a puddle,' he said, 'down the kerb.'

'Hang on,' said Jack.

He brought over the black builder's bucket he used for carrying water, tools, or sand. The ubiquitous container.

'Wring your socks out.'

Deneb hesitated, then shrugged, took them off, one at a time, and wrung them into the bucket. Dirty water oozed out. When he'd done, he hung the damp socks on the rail of the chair Phil had vacated. Jack handed him some sheets of paper towel. Deneb wiped his feet, separating his toes and underfoot.

Jack took the bucket, and headed out the back, tipping the bucket into the sink into the rear, giving the bucket a quick rinse. Don't rush things, he'd learnt. Establish trust.

His phone buzzed. He glanced at the screen, a message from George Taplow. What had the man to say? Go jump in the lake, or what? He hadn't expected such a quick answer. In fact, he had been prepared for none at all.

Jack read the message. It was a clear yes, saying Taplow would be in at 5pm and prepared to talk about his ex-wife. He gave his home address in Stratford.

Well, well. He needed to think about this. Had he been too hasty contacting Taplow? It would blow any chance with Penny, if she found out. No second chances.

Why did he have to be so distrusting?

First things first. Deal with Deneb, then he'd message Taplow, apologise and cancel. Musing on this, Jack collected the cups and the tray in the shop and took them into the office.

'We have a client, I think,' he said to Mia, 'or maybe we have one, not sure yet. I don't like to keep asking you, but can you make another cuppa.'

She grimaced. 'I'm not your skivvy!'

'He got very wet,' said Jack. 'And there's no heat in this place. Apart from your blow heater.'

'Do you want it?'

'No.'

Mia weighed up the request. 'I am not going to continually make tea. That's not why I left school.'

'Fair enough.'

He picked up the kettle, felt its weight. Sufficient, probably. He plugged it in.

And left the office.

Such were quarrels, starting with the petty, who made the tea. And ending in divorce.

Jack came back into the shop and, taking the other chair, sat down opposite Deneb. Weird. A man in paint stained overalls posing as a detective. Wrong clothing, wrong scenery.

'Have you any legal qualifications?' Deneb said.

'None at all.'

'So what is a private investigator?'

'Also called private detective, a sleuth, a tec, a dick, a private eye, a gumshoe.' He and Mia had gone through the thesaurus. 'He or she investigates anything the client wants investigated. Could be crime, or what a husband or wife is up to, financial mismanagement, that sort of thing.'

He needed a better list. Job for Mia. What PIs do. Better than making tea.

'Do you need any qualifications to become one?' said Deneb.

Jack was puzzled at where this was going.

He said, 'None. You make a website, put a company name on your office door, get some cards printed, and hope you can get clients.'

'So anybody could call themselves a private investigator?'

Jack nodded. 'It's utterly unregulated. No official body. To be honest, I am new to the game. I have helped the police a number of times. I seem to have a head for sorting things out, but I don't have any paper qualifications. In fact, if you want someone with a diploma in private investigations, then I am not your man.'

Was he being too honest? He didn't really know what was being asked, the underlying reason for Deneb's interrogation. Mia had said, you have to pretend that you are experienced, tell the client that you have a portfolio of cases, though how she would know any more than he did... For himself, he reckoned, you get the feel of the person you are talking to, and then decide whether to tell the truth or spin a line.

There was Phil, a little earlier, Jack had lied to him. All that client confidentiality codswallop. When there was no client of his on the walk. But he felt no need to do this to Deneb. Perhaps he was clever than Jack was.

'I am not who you think I am,' said Deneb.

At last, it was coming out, the reason why Deneb had stayed and had given him the once over.

'Who are you?' he said.

'My name was Adam. I won't tell you my second name, then you won't know, should you ever be questioned. And Adam is a very common name.' He hesitated, then said, 'It's difficult to know where to start. I have never told anyone this before. You spoke of client confidentiality. I expect this of you.'

'I will not tell anyone what you are about to tell me.'

That seemed to satisfy Deneb. He nodded.

'All my papers were lost in the Channel. My wife and son too. I have told you this.' Jack nodded. 'As a student, after graduating in Damascus, I went to Berkeley, California for further study. There, I became friends with another Syrian whose name was Deneb. We looked a little alike, you know short, brown skinned, clean shaven, with the same sort of English accent. We were often confused with one another. For a while, we worked together in the same department. He was a few years older than me. More experienced, he had published papers in English in various publications. He was well regarded. I loved him like a brother.'

'You somehow took over his identity,' said Jack, running ahead.

'Yes. We both went back to Damascus from Berkeley, and worked in the physics department at the University. He was my boss. Then the war started. Deneb got too involved, he fought for the losing side, and one day he disappeared. Thousands did, still do. The military or the police picked him up and nothing has been heard of him since. That was ten years ago. He could be in prison, but I doubt it. Why should they keep him so long? The torture and conditions would kill anyone in a very few years.'

'Why did you become him?'

'I had to stay in the UK. The Home Office are very stringent. Deneb had papers published, I had nothing to my name. I wouldn't say he was famous but he was well regarded. Talking to a few people in the transit camp in Kent, before my interviews, I got the lie of the land. And once the interviews began, I told them I was Deneb Ali. They didn't believe me, but then they don't believe anyone. Prove it, they always say. So I referred them to Berkeley. That didn't work, until I managed to get a solicitor, Miriam, a wonderful Jewish lady, I think I might have mentioned her to you.' Jack nodded. 'She contacted Berkeley, and as I told you, they were always confusing the two of us, and I knew enough about Deneb to convince Berkeley who gave me an excellent reference. And the Home Office accepted me. I had troubles, minor ones you might say, once I had permission to stay, getting a place to live and work. I had to study all the hours God sends to be Deneb. But I managed it. I burnt the midnight oil. I had no family to tell me to go to bed. I read, I copied things down, went through the mathematics line by line of his papers.' He stopped, hoping he had made his point. 'I have had papers published myself. I have become Deneb Ali.'

'You are worried that Mike's murder might result in you getting found out.'

'I am. We are all suspects. And if they look closely enough, they could find out I am not Deneb Ali.'

'You fooled the Home Office. So why are you so concerned?'

'Because I didn't fool Mike Rayner. He didn't like immigrants, well those with brown skins anyway, and boat people especially. He didn't like me being in the walking group. I thought of leaving the group, but I stayed as I loved the walking, and I am a private person. One group was enough for me to try. Mike was an awful person. I had no idea what he was doing. It turns out, he got a private detective investigating me who found out who I really was. Don't ask me how he did it. Don't ask me how good the evidence is. I don't know. Whether Mike was stretching something because he hated what I represent, I don't know. On Saturday's walk I was going to try to convince him that I am truly Deneb. Bribery was out of the question. He is fifty times richer than me.' Deneb shrugged, his narrative all out. 'So, there you have it. Who I am and what I am afraid of.'

Jack thought, what does he want from me? I am not a priest. How can I help him? And then realised how he could. The only way forward.

'If the police find out I am a fraud,' said Deneb, 'let's not call it anything else, they will either convict me of Mike's murder or I will be deported as I have lied to the Home Office.' He hesitated a few seconds, then added, 'If they send back to Syria, I too will disappear.'

Mia appeared with three cups of tea on her tray.

'Oh, I thought there were three of you.'

'One left ten minutes ago. We'll manage the extra,' said Jack. 'Thanks.' He had forgotten about the kettle. Their tiff. He must make the tea some of the time.

Deneb gratefully accepted his tea and sugared it.

Mia said, 'Let me have your socks and boots. I'll put them by the heater.'

Deneb handed them over.

'Thank you, my dear. I am grateful for your concern.'

'All part of the service,' she said, and smiled, for the client and her father.

She left them.

'Thank you for confiding in me,' said Jack. 'I will not tell anyone what you've told me. Client confidentiality.' As he said it, he thought, I sound like a priest, the confessional, however that worked. 'If Queen Mary University accept you as the physicist Deneb Ali, who am I to argue?'

'It's not the university, but the police,' said Deneb, 'their criminal investigation, I fear.'

'We must find out who the murderer is,' he said. 'And do so, before they get too deep into the inquiry. Once they have arrested him or her, they'll have no interest in the other suspects.'

Chapter 23

'Our first client,' said Mia, clapping her hands.

They were in the office, where Jack appreciated the warmth of the blow heater. It was smelly in the small room, the remnant of Deneb's socks and boots, the articles gone with the owner's exit. Bearable for Jack, he had been in mess huts far smellier than this, with many more dirty boots and socks on big building sites.

Jack had made them tea, knowing he had to keep up his score.

'We are employed to find the killer of Mike Rayner,' he said.

'You were working on it, anyway,' she said.

'Simmering on the back burner,' he said. 'Now it's on the front, high light.'

'And he saw the website. Great.' She peered at her father. 'See? I can do more than make tea.'

'I never doubted it, partner.'

Mia was behind the desk with her laptop, she did so remind him of her mother, Alison, apart from her wild hair. Alison was groomed and smart. Mia dressed to suit her anarchism.

'How much have you charged him?' she said.

Jack shrugged, uncomfortably. 'We didn't talk money.'

Mia threw up her hands, aghast.

'No wonder we are in the poorhouse!' She shook both hands in annoyance. 'You wouldn't do that with a building client. You'd have given a quote.'

He had to agree.

'So how come you let him go without talking money?'

Jack thought on it. Why had he been so unprofessional?

He said, 'All the other investigations, I did for nothing.'

'For fun,' she said bitingly.

'So money didn't cross my mind,' he said, ignoring her sarcasm. 'And this was so complicated. His situation just filled my head totally.'

There were no excuses, really. As a builder, first and foremost, with any job was getting payment. It had not even been a vestige with Deneb's plight. He liked the man, sympathised with his dilemma, had been enveloped by it.

All the excuses of an amateur.

'Give me his contact details and I'll send him a list of our fees,' said Mia.

Jack had no counter arguments. She was right. Surprisingly so, for an eco-warrior-cum-socialist.

'Welcome to capitalism,' he said.

She grimaced at the charge. 'We have a right to make a living, Dad. We are not exploiting the man, just telling him what we charge. Does he work for nothing?'

Jack had to agree that Queen Mary University probably paid him quite well. He didn't know how much. It wasn't his world. Deneb wasn't a professor like Penny, but he got a regular salary and had a cheap flat from the college, no family commitments, sadly. So yes, Deneb was solvent.

He gave her the contact details, more than willing to hand over the task.

'Have you heard from George Taplow?' she said.

'Yes.' He hesitated a moment before adding, 'He said he'd be free at 5 pm.'

'That's good.'

'I'm wondering whether to go or not.'

She said, leaning forward, 'You have a case to solve, we are getting paid for it. Taplow is Penny's ex, and she's a suspect in the murder.'

Mia knew more or less what occurred on the walk, all but Nova's undercover role, which he'd pledged to keep secret.

'I am going out with Penny,' he said, trying to excuse his hesitation.

Was he actually going out with her? A pizza parlour, a walk and its consequences, the interviews. Did that amount to dating? Or the prelude to it? But whatever.

'I don't want to blow it,' he said.

Mia guffawed. That stung somewhat. Trivialising his needs.

'Conflict,' she declared, clapping her hands. 'I love it!'

'If Penny finds out I'm talking to her ex-husband, that's the end of our relationship,' he said, uncomfortable at revealing such details to his daughter, but work partner too, though their working roles had not been formalised.

'I won't be telling her,' said Mia. 'And you won't be. Plus we have a client.' She thumped the table. 'You have to go and talk to Taplow.'

'Might be a waste of time.'

'Might not be.'

Jack had been coming to this reluctant conclusion himself. But Mia had fixed it for him. He had to see the man, just to know if he could add anything to the holes in the narrative.

He went back to work.

For an hour or so, Jack worked on the counter frames. At 3:30, it was agreed, he should go home and smarten up for his first professional interview. Mia would lock up.

At 3:30 prompt, he threw her the keys.

'Wish me luck.'

She gave him the thumbs up. And Jack left the shop.

Chapter 24

At home, Jack had a rapid shower. Wandering about in his underwear, he considered what to wear for the interview. He put on his only suit, worn for weddings and funerals, and stood before the mirror in the bathroom, the only one long enough. Turning this way and that, he felt like a con man or a banker. And hedge fund manager.

And took off the suit.

What do private detectives wear? He knew them mostly through movies and TV series. Humphrey Bogart as Philip Marlowe wore a crumpled suit and a homburg hat. Sherlock Holmes a deerstalker and suit, Poirot, a suit, waistcoat and pocket watch. Even James Bond, not a private eye at all, but a government secret agent, had a posh suit.

Not for him.

For hats, Jack had the choice of a woolly beanie or a flat cap. What did they say about him? Mia would tell him. But she wasn't here to add her three-penn'orth.

When married, he would protest at Alison when she took ages getting ready for an occasion, and here he was, in angst about what to wear.

Why were appearances so important?

Because of what people thought. Their image of what a private investigator is. As confused as his own, a jumble of suits and deerstalkers.

Jack settled for the trousers of his suit, so half respectable, a casual shirt. He certainly was not going to wear a tie. That's what the foreman wore. Flat cap, that would do. Shoes would have been a difficulty, if he'd had many pairs. But the choice was limited to a pair of work boots, a pair of trainers and some dress shoes that he hardly ever wore if he could help it, and certainly not today. So it was trainers, like it or not.

Surely it was all down to confidence. Except he didn't feel at all confident. And then his wheels. The big joke. All he had was his van, with *Jack of All Trades* plastered on both sides. That was him to a T.

Master of none.

Unsuitably attired, Jack drove to Stratford.

Taplow lived in one of the high rise blocks in the Olympic Park. Most of the blocks had been part of the 2012 Olympic village. None of which had kitchens at the time, as the athletes ate in dining halls, so there was a major refit when the London Olympics were over. One of the bedrooms was made into a kitchen, baths put in and not just showers. He'd had mates involved in the refits, lots of work going for plumbers, electricians and builders. Once completed, the private blocks were sold off to the Qatari Royal Family, and, what was left, to various housing associations who set more reasonable rents.

Getting to the Olympic Park was straightforward. Then it got tricky. Jack had to use his phone to navigate the maze of streets in the Olympic Park, having no satnav in his ancient vehicle. Stopping, starting, the minutes ticked by. He got out to check a couple of times on the site boards.

And arrived, a little flustered, a few minutes late. The block was about ten stories, Taplow up on the ninth, and must be earning a fair whack to have one of these apartments.

What did he do for a living?

Jack locked the van. Hardly necessary as there were choicer vehicles on the road, then again, his was easier to get into. He took a deep breath. Be calm. Or at least look the part.

He said to himself three times, 'Jack Bell, Private Investigator.' He held out a card to an invisible client, which said *Jack Bell, Private Investigator, Forest Gate Investigations,* with his phone and website, and vine leaves around the edge. A Mia Bell design.

He pressed the buzzer.

'Who is it?'

'Jack Bell, private investigator.'

The first time he'd used the title to a real person, as opposed to a brick wall. Deneb had assumed he was what his website said. What a fraud.

'Please come up.'

Jack was buzzed in. A concierge, or whatever you called her, sat at a desk. That must up the rent somewhat. She gave him a smile and he managed one back. And went to the lifts. A door of one of the two was open, he stepped in and pushed the button for the ninth floor.

One wall was mirrored, and he looked himself over. The flat cap made him look like a taxi driver. He took it off and put it in his anorak pocket. He had a notebook and pen in the other.

Out of the lift, his shoes crackled on the carpet. Electrostatic, dry as dust up here in the heat. Too hot. That costs too. His hair prickled at his neck. Along the hallway, a stocky black man was waiting at the door of an apartment.

Jack approached him, a spark or two flying. A strange effect, he hadn't witnessed before. Too much wasted heat.

'Mr Taplow,' he enquired, as he got to the man.

'That's me.'

'Jack Bell. Private Investigator.'

He was almost used to the job title.

'You want to talk to me about my ex-wife, Penny Hicks?'

'Can we go inside?' said Jack, indicating the open door.

'No,' said Taplow.

That was a surprise. He'd expected to be sitting down, perhaps offered tea, not stood in a hot, electrostatically charged hallway.

'This interview will be short,' went on Taplow. 'My girlfriend is inside and I don't want to disturb her. So we'll have our chat out here. Please tell me why you want to know about Penny.'

'She is a suspect in the murder of Mike Rayner.'

'And why are you, a private investigator, investigating. Surely it is a police matter?'

The interrogator being interrogated. Not a good start. Jack had got nothing out of Taplow beyond his appearance. A black man, very short hair, clean shaven, possibly did weight training by his build, wearing a pale grey suit with a shirt, but no tie, slippers. And quite forceful.

And well off, to live here.

'The police are investigating,' said Jack, 'but they are very slow.' He had no idea whether they were or not, but had to justify his presence. 'And my client wishes to move things on.'

'Who is your client?'

Here we go. He took a deep breath.

'I'm afraid I can't tell you.'

'So why should I answer any of your questions?'

He was getting nowhere. Stuck out in the hallway, he was being questioned, not the other way round.

'I am hoping we can eliminate Penny as a suspect.' That at least was true.

'No good, Mr Bell. You have come here out of the blue...'

'I emailed you,' he said. 'You said I could come.'

'And you want to delve into my past.'

He was interrupted by a woman's voice from inside the flat.

'Who is it, dear?'

She appeared in the hallway. A slim, black woman with purple lipstick, hair in small black plaits. Well, well.

'How's Marcus Garvey?' said Jack.

She came to the door, stared at him. 'You're Jack!' she cried. 'On the walk, Saturday.'

'Good to see you, Fiona.'

He hoped it was good. Couldn't be worse.

'I'm glad you two know each other,' said Taplow.

'He was on that walk, that short, eventful walk,' said Fiona. 'And my cat is fine, thank you.'

'Did you know Jack is a private investigator?'

She had an intake of breath. 'I did not.' She glared at him. 'What were you doing on the walk, Jack?'

A direct challenge. They were a tough pair. Well suited, perhaps. Or fighting like cats and dogs.

'I was investigating Mike,' he said, immediately realising he'd need to be sharp to keep that ball in the air. 'Let's go inside. And I'll put you in the picture.'

Fiona and Taplow looked to each other, at Jack's assertiveness, but curiosity won out.

'Come inside,' said Taplow.

Jack followed them into the apartment. He had needed a good tale, to get them talking. To find out about Penny. But saying he was a private eye investigating Mike? He had needed something on the hoof. Yes, it had got him in the flat, but might yet sink him as he could barely think out the why's and wherefore's of that scenario.

A short hallway led into a long sitting room. There was a curved sofa, with a paisley pattern, that would maybe seat five, two armchairs to match, and matching drapes at the windows, almost overpowering him in paisley. Between the drapes, outside, was the balustrade of a balcony, beyond, in the distance, the crown of what was once the Olympic Stadium, and now the West Ham ground. On the white walls of the room were three large abstract paintings that Nova could tell him about but meant nothing to Jack beyond colour and a jumble of pattern. There was a large TV, a highly polished dining table with chairs, and books on glass shelves in an alcove. All too tidy and too different from his sloppy, cheaper lifestyle, to be comfortable.

It was hot too. Jack had taken off his anorak. If on his own, he'd have stripped down to his t-shirt.

'Please sit down,' said Taplow.

Jack sat on the sofa, Taplow sat on the arm of one of the armchairs, Fiona joined Jack on the sofa, but as far away as she could be. He threw his anorak on the back of the sofa. Taplow grimaced, was about to say something at the territorial infringement, but swallowed it.

They were waiting on him.

It was good technique, he'd learnt working with the police. Be silent and wait. Discomfort often forced mistakes. But he needed to take the lead.

He turned to Fiona. 'What did you do at the snack break during the walk?'

She snorted. 'You were going to tell us about investigating Mike.'

'It's all of a piece,' he said. 'My investigation, the murder, who was doing what. Just let me ask a few questions, and then I'll answer yours.'

'Why?' said Taplow.

'Because so far, you have told me nothing, but bombarded me with questions.'

'Your being here is questionable,' said Taplow.

'George,' said Fiona putting up a pacifying hand. 'Let's play the game.'

Taplow took a deep breath, as if deciding whether to continue his attack, or backtrack. Fiona waved her hands to quell his attack. He nodded, somewhat reluctantly.

'You want to know about Penny and me?' he said.

'I do,' said Jack, though noting that his question to Fiona had been left hanging.

'During our two years of marriage, she never ever attacked me with a knife. Threw china yes, and words which felt like knives, but no hard steel. She was too self-centred, too independent, too argumentative. At the beginning, I found her immensely attractive, but by the end, I'd rather have slept with a shark.'

There was a marriage turned to dross. Jack would have liked to defend Penny, saying he'd found her good company, but he was here to listen, not set up a row over Penny's qualities.

'She could be a cow,' said Fiona.

'Did you row with Penny?' he said to her.

'Frequently.'

'Over what?'

Fiona shrugged. 'White and black matters. Slavery in the British Empire. White feminism.'

'You are with Mr Taplow...' he began.

'George,' said Taplow, though not indicating friendliness.

'You are with George,' he went on, unsure how to phrase it, 'how did that fit with Penny?'

'You mean did I steal George from her?' She gave a half laugh. 'There was no one but George in the bed when I arrived.'

There were too many questions bubbling away, with Fiona, with Taplow, about Penny, about who was doing what on the walk. He could barely think straight in this hostile space.

They were waiting on him once more.

'At the snack break on the walk,' he returned to the unanswered query, 'what did you do?'

'I played my penny whistle. Not that well. I was nervous, first time I'd played in public. Silly really. I talked to Penny before that.'

'In spite of the fact, she could be a cow, and you argued over black and white matters?'

'She tested me,' said Fiona. 'Penny is sharp, logical, prejudiced to be sure, I've never met a white woman who wasn't. But she makes a good argument. I can respect that. I like a skilful sword fight with a practised opponent. We talked about the silly dispute I'd had with Phil about whether there could be a black Alice in a movie. Penny and I had a common enemy. Penny was OK with mixed casting. Then she left me and went over to talk to you, seeing you all alone. You were messing about with a yogurt pot, if I recall.'

'I had forgotten my spoon, and was making one from the lid.'

'I watched you, as I played. You were very involved. But all considered, very neglectful.'

'Of what?'

'Of Mike. Your quarry. He wanders off and, instead of following the man you have been paid to shadow, you make a spoon.'

'I had no idea what was going to happen.'

'A poor reply,' Taplow guffawed. 'If you knew what was going to happen, why go at all?'

'I was hungry,' said Jack. Aware that he was indeed inept, that is if he had in reality been a private eye watching Mike, but he didn't want to be waylaid and let Fiona off the hook. 'Penny came over to talk to me while I made my spoon,' he continued, hoping there'd be no interruption. 'What did you do then?'

'Enough penny whistle, I then contemplated who might play Alice in a movie.' She smiled. 'Her hairdo, her dress, her nails. I thought the caterpillar might be a stoned Rasta, with a spliff instead of a hookah, the Red Queen would be Margaret Thatcher. The playing cards would be shackled, a chain gang or plantation slaves.' She stopped, and gave a satisfied grin. 'On a walk, you don't have to chat all the time.'

'Why were you investigating Mike?' said Taplow. He hadn't moved from his position on the arm of the chair, giving himself a higher stance, while Jack was sunk in the sofa.

This was it, he thought. The big one; it had got him in the flat, but he could no longer parry it away. He must construct a tale that made sense to these heavy inquisitors.

'He was buying and selling stolen paintings.' Straight in at the deep end.

'How do you know?'

'Contacts,' said Jack. Which was true as far as it went. A thought hit him. 'You are an art dealer, George. Aren't you?'

'I am.' Taplow smiled. 'And you are more astute than you appear, Jack. But you could do better than those trainers and that anorak. If you'll take my advice.'

He was looking at Jack's somewhat scruffy shoes. They were out of place in this room. Jack would get no employment here.

Ignoring the jibe, Jack went on, 'Did you ever buy paintings from Mike Rayner?'

There was a pause, too long. Fiona looked at Taplow who nodded.

'I think we have said all that we are going to say,' said Taplow.

He rose.

'I'll see you to the lift,' said Fiona, rising.

It was obvious, the interview was at an end. Jack picked up his anorak and threw it over his shoulder. He wished he could photograph the pictures on the wall. Not likely they were stolen, but you never knew. And there were connections, a circuit board of them, if only he could figure where the wires went. Taplow an art dealer, in the same realm as Mike Rayner. And Fiona here, the two, it seemed in cahoots.

What was all this about?

As Jack and Fiona walked away from the flat, down the corridor, Taplow stayed at the apartment door, watching them on the long carpet to the lift. As if he didn't trust Fiona, as well as Jack.

She said quietly, when they were some way from her lover, 'Take care, Jack. You are getting into deep water.'

'How deep?'

'Deep enough to drown in.'

They had come to the lift. She pressed the button.

'I've been thinking who your client might be,' she said. 'It doesn't make sense for it to be one of the walking group. Not if Mike was your quarry.'

'I can't say who it is.'

At least, he could hide under that shroud. And not say, no one at all, I was just on a walk. Though he had a client now, but certainly not then. He had simply come along with Penny.

'But why are you questioning me?' she exclaimed. She prodded him in the chest. 'About Mike's murder. You seem to be riding two horses.'

The lift had arrived. The door opened. Jack stepped in.

As the door closed, Fiona put her foot in it.

'Are you really a private eye?'

Good question, he thought, giving her the card he had kept in his trouser pocket for just such an occasion. She glanced at it, took her foot out of the door, and it closed. He quickly pressed the button for the ground floor. And sank against the wall as the lift began to descend.

Chapter 25

Once out of the block, Jack went at once to his van and drove off. As if his weariness and his lies could be picked up through the fabric of the building. Like emanations from a séance, the misty tentacles making their way through the brickwork to Taplow and Fiona's detector.

He stopped about quarter of a mile away, far enough, still in the Olympic Park, among its tower blocks, but out of sight from Taplow and Fiona's. Was she living there, or was she just a frequent visitor?

Jack scrawled a few notes so he'd remember later, being unable to write anything in the hurly burly of the meeting. Or rather non-meeting, his mind had been pulling free of its tether, thrashing in a wind of words.

He should have asked about the penny whistle. So much said. So much to be sorted out.

But he'd learnt a little more about Penny. That Taplow hated his ex but she had never attacked him with a knife, Fiona sometimes hated her, and sometimes respected her. And at the snack break, Penny had been talking with Fiona before coming over to him on his log, toying with the spoon lid.

What had he been hoping for?

A pointer from Taplow on his ex-wife. But the headline wasn't about Penny at all. She was on page two, you might say, a single column with the front page splash being Fiona shacked up with art dealer Taplow, a real shocker. As soon as Jack pressed him further on art dealing, he was shown the door.

Jack had walked into the lion's den, and had walked out again, still with four limbs and a head. He had learnt a muddle of things. How on earth did they all connect? What would happen if this meeting ever got back to Penny? And then a thought, and a chuckle over his cunning. He would say to her that he had gone to see Fiona, and was surprised to find Taplow there.

But how would he know Fiona was there. Besides which, Penny and he were due to see Fiona tomorrow night. Penny would want to know why he had broken ranks.

Didn't he trust her, she might say?

Lying was hard work. Difficult to keep the untruths consistent. Though lying seemed part of the job. Jack was playing too many parts, with the play still being written. He was one of the walkers, he was dating Penny, he was something or other with Nova, he was a private eye with a client who had been on the walk. Of course, the roles crossed over and slashed each other out.

What to do now?

He would like to sleep for a week, but that wasn't on the cards. Nor would he sleep, he was too hyper. Things needed sorting out, the muddle of threads, as if a kitten had been at the ball of wool, and the beginning and end couldn't be found, the strand twisted in and out of everything else.

Why not see Liz?

It was only a ten minute run down to her place. That's if she would talk to him after last time's hurried exit. She'd been affronted when they had asked her if she had killed Mike. He grinned to himself. What a sloppy question. Not worth asking. If she had, she would not admit it. And her anger over it, had told them nothing. It was either a put on or genuine. Even lie detectors couldn't tell you which.

Jack drove out of the Olympic Park, heading towards the Stratford ring road. It was rush hour, a little after six o'clock. Might be a long ten minutes. Traffic clogged just before the Theatre Royal. He could just go home, but he'd pushed the Liz button, and had begun thinking about her.

Eventually out of the ring road, and alongside St John's church and down West Ham Lane. All known territory.

Feeling better, breathing more freely with every yard away from Taplow and Fiona and their two-pronged attack.

Drive and breathe.

Stop start in the traffic, no matter. This was a cold call, she'd either be in or not. He was not late or early. He just happened to be passing, and thought he'd pop in, as one does. As he hardly ever did.

The traffic wasn't too bad along the Barking Road. Could be worse, would be worse. All the traffic, that Mia cursed, the cacophony of machines carbonising the air we breathe, boiling the world. Rush hour said it all. Too loudly, too oily.

Jack parked in the area below Liz's block, and was locking up, when he saw her leaving.

He waved, calling out, 'Liz!'

She was at the door of the block, looking about to see who was shouting her name. She wore a half length green coat, quite different from her khaki shorts and loose top she had worn on the walk, a matching beret, a yellow silk scarf, and red lipstick.

What was she? Seventy-five, give or take.

Jack walked rapidly over.

'Come back for another volley of grapeshot, have you?' she said as he got to her.

'A chat,' he said. 'No accusations.'

'Do you know who the murderer is yet?'

'I don't,' he said. And that was certainly true.

'You still think it could be me.'

He hesitated, and she laughed.

'I'm going for a coffee,' she said. 'I am fed up with my four walls. Buy me one and I'll talk to you.'

She took his arm. 'People will think you are my toy boy,' she said with a mischievous grin.

Jack reflected, as they walked arm in arm, it was a sort of mock flirting. She was pleased to be with someone half her age. Almost a boy in her eyes. And probably why she would talk to him.

Sex opens doors.

Chapter 26

The coffee shop, just off Rathbone Market, was quite busy, but they found a table for two. The shop would be closing in half an hour, and the baristas were cleaning up behind the counter. Joni Mitchell's song *Both Sides Now* was playing in the background.

How can you look at clouds from both sides? But he wished they'd turn it up. What did he know about clouds, anyway? Agreeing with the singer. Then again, why would you want to know about clouds, unless you were a weatherman?

Though some might say, what about meteor showers or the craters on the moon?

Back with their order, Jack put the coffee and cakes on the table, and put a hand to his ear. 'I'm listening,' he said to Liz, held by the voice, the lyrics, the sparkling guitar. Mia had said it was liquid poetry. Soul music. It touched him, Joni's ignorance on cloud matters.

Perhaps she should go to the library.

The track changed, one of those annoying compilations, when he wanted another Joni Mitchell. Perhaps as well. He hadn't come here to listen to music, but had questions to ask. Their last interview with Liz, his and Penny's, had gone badly. He wondered would it have been so, if it had just been him.

So important who asks the questions.

At the table, with coffee and cake, Jack tried a question about her daughter in Spain, making it as unthreatening, off the cuff as he could, as he'd surmised there was something hidden under the carpet. But it was brushed aside and, all at once, unasked, she was telling him about her daughter Ellie in Australia. Ellie had married a sheep farmer in New South Wales. Some other time, he might have got interested in the thousand acres and the five hundred sheep, or was it the other ways round, the eucalyptus and koalas, kangaroos and dingoes, what the rabbits were doing to the wheat, and the wild fire that just missed the farm. An article, he might have read in the paper, or skipped for the sport.

A little later, he tried again with Gill in Spain, and Liz bounced it away, going on about West Ham this season. How they'd just lost to Everton of all teams. The manager was useless, and had to go. Two of their best players had been transferred. This was so predictable, she went on, a six year old could do better. Jack half entered the conversation, it was of interest, but just not now. Liz though had taken charge: wind her up and she could talk for England, bringing home the gold medal and the team cup.

Not content with Australia and West Ham, she began asking Jack questions, about his early life, not far from here. Schooling, marriage, his daughter. At which point, he knew, he couldn't bring her back to what he wanted to ask. The only point of him being here. Liz was happy. A toy boy buying her coffee, listening and answering her questions.

She nudged his knee with hers.

Jack reflected on interviews. The who, when and how of them. Those at the police station, with the arrested man questioned. In the interview room, the man not allowed to question the cops back. The suspect could remain silent, he could say 'no comment' to every question or spill the beans on the rest of the gang. But if he tried to question the interviewer, the proceedings would be halted. Against the rules, which they had made. One way traffic only.

Or the journalist out for a story. The celeb eager to tell her side, and the journalist either taking it as gospel, as that's what their readers wanted, or attempting to dig further, both with jobs to do. Or the press posse, door-stopping a beleaguered woman about her errant husband, a cabinet minister say, caught with his trousers down. Shouts through her letterbox, incessant phone calls, while she turns off the lights and hides under the kitchen table.

You win some, you lose some, he thought of this one. No wonder tabloids made up stories. He, she and the cat won't give the answers you want, so write it up anyway. Only the rich can afford to sue; the poor must suffer whatever is flung at them.

Liz had stopped, she must have said something meaningful. To her, at least.

'Sorry,' he said. 'I didn't catch that.'

Was it kangaroos in the outback or the West Ham manager's peccadilloes?

'Another coffee?' she said, lifting her empty mug.

A simple question, with a simple let out.

'I've really got to go,' said Jack, looking at his watch as if that told him something he hadn't known.

He rose, kissed Liz on the cheek.

'My daughter is making dinner tonight,' he said. 'Something special. Her birthday. I promised her I'd be back by seven.'

White lies, whatever they may be. In his case, I've had more than enough of this nowhere chat.

Liz thanked him for the coffee and cake, saying he was welcome to call when he was around this way.

Chapter 27

Mia had made a salad with walnuts and chickpeas. He had given her a tenner before he'd gone out, to get some food in.

'You don't have to eat it, if you don't want it,' she said, seeing her father's expression.

'Looks good,' he said. Not much of a lie.

'It's vegan,' she said. 'Minimal attack on the planet.' She handed him the dressing. 'So, how did it go with Taplow?'

Jack told her that Fiona had been there too. And the pair had harried him mercilessly.

He said, 'Could you find out if she is living there?'

'Why?'

'It will tell us how close they are.'

Mia thought for a few seconds. 'Be tricky, but I'll have a go.'

Jack was filling up with bread, having eaten most of the salad. The problem with the vegan diet, it had something missing. The meat drug.

'I popped down to see Liz,' he said, between mouthfuls. 'I learnt all about her daughter's sheep farm, and how awful the West Ham manager is. And not much else.' He took a swig of tea, oat milk, not so bad. 'I tried asking about her daughter in Spain, but every time, she changed the subject. Gill Greene. How's your Spanish?'

'I've done half the Advanced level course,' she said.

'Do you want to see what you can find out?'

'Be interesting to see if my Spanish is up to it. And there's Google Translate to help out. Could get into that. Any idea how old she is? What part of Spain?'

'Barcelona. I'd say she was late 20s, early 30s.'

They finished the meal; the rule was whoever didn't cook washed up. Mia tended to go overboard with dirty bowls and plates. They had a dishwasher, but it was just for show. Something wrong with the electrics. He should get someone round some day.

Jack's phone rang.

It was Alison, Mia's mother.

'Can I talk to Mia?' she said, when they were past the greetings. 'She doesn't answer her phone.'

'Your mother.' Jack held out the phone. Mia reluctantly took it.

'I'll talk to you if you stop telling me off,' she said, into the phone, and went into the sitting room.

Jack washed most of the dishes. There was always a point when he got bored with the task. Tomorrow was another day. More dishes and more dishes. The entropy of everyday life.

Nova was coming at 8pm. He hoped Penny had forgotten or was working late. Or anything.

Jack changed his suit trousers for jeans. The trousers, paired again with the jacket, could wait for the next funeral. He made tea for his thermos, his part in their night time picnic, and put it in his backpack, with woollies for chilly autumn evenings. He took his telescope out and put it in his van, so he'd be ready for a quick getaway when Nova arrived.

She was on time, ringing him, saying she was outside waiting.

Jack said to Mia, 'If Penny comes say I've got a customer in Seven Kings.'

Mia nodded, still on the phone with her mother, rolling her eyes to indicate Alison was going on and on.

'Got to dash,' exclaimed Jack.

He heaved on his backpack, and took the stairs two at time, to get away from the house as quickly as he could.

Before anyone else arrived.

PART THREE:
OVER THE FLATS

Chapter 28

Nova was bundled up in scarf, yellow woolly hat and red anorak, and he noted, her walking boots, the ones she'd worn on the fateful day. She had a backpack, presumably with pizza and some other goodies. He was limited to drinks, the thermos and two cups.

Nova had driven to his place, but they took Jack's van for the journey to the Flats. With the telescope in the back, the routine was to put it and the mount into his wheelbarrow, once parked, and push it to the favoured site on the Flats.

As they were heading off, she said:

'Busy?'

'Shop work,' he said, and couldn't help saying, 'and interviews for a client.'

'Got some detective work then?'

'Yes.'

They turned onto Woodgrange Road, going in the opposite direction from the shop he was working in, past the Co-op and the station, where the walkers had met on Saturday, driving down towards the Flats.

'Do you know who Fiona is shacked up with?' he said. He knew the answer, but what did Nova know, being part of the walking group.

He slowed where the road narrowed on the way to the second station in Forest Gate, Wanstead Park. A cyclist was in front of them, without lights.

'I'd pick him, if I was on duty,' she said indicating the cyclist. Then added, 'Fiona has moved in with George

Taplow, Penny's ex-husband. She has sold her flat, so can't go back if it doesn't work out. Risky, don't you think?'

Jack was irritated that she knew more than he did. He had wanted to tell her, proving that private investigator weren't just words on his card.

'How did you find out?'

She shrugged. 'I moved in art dealer circles, with you know whom. Taplow and Fiona were at a private viewing that I went to with Mike. Fiona a little embarrassed at me being there. She didn't know I was a cop, but as a fellow club member. She asked me not to tell anyone. Taplow let slip, she had moved in, and later on, I checked on her property. Just sold.' She stopped for a few seconds as they went under the railway bridge, a train rumbling overhead. Once out of the bridge noise, she added, 'Taplow is a player of significance in the art world.'

'Could've told you that,' he said, miffed that he hadn't. Not that he knew that Fiona had moved in with Taplow, but she had certainly had every appearance of being more than an occasional visitor.

The Flats were in sight, the sky ahead cloudy. They were hoping for a few clear patches to spot the odd planet and shooting stars.

'Can I assume your client is connected with Mike's murder?' she said.

'Assume what you like,' he said. 'Client confidentiality.'

Even as he said it, he wondered on the wisdom of cutting her off. The cops had access to all sorts of information which he couldn't get himself. And although she had been taken off the investigation, she could find out where it was at without much hassle.

Jack said, 'Deneb Ali is my client.'

And wished he hadn't, as Deneb had faked his identity, and he didn't want the cops getting wind of it. Too late, but at least Nova wasn't part of the investigating team.

He turned into Capel Road, slowing down as they bumped over the sleeping policeman. Not worried about himself, but the sensitive passenger in the rear, wrapped in a blanket, not wanting to risk a cracked lens.

'Why Deneb?' she said.

He took a line out of Mia's playbook.

'He reckons racist cops will pin it on a convenient BAME in the group.'

Jack was looking for a parking space as he drove slowly down the road that lined the Flats.

'That leaves Fiona too,' she said helpfully. Then added, 'I am sure the rest are not off the hook.'

He pulled into a space.

'Does that include me and you?' he said.

'You,' she said. 'Not me. I was working.'

Jack wondered. He hadn't considered Nova a suspect. But on the walk, she had told the group that Mike wasn't answering in his phone. Having done the deed, it was OK to get them finding the corpse. But why might she kill him?

Jack turned motives over as they loaded the telescope into his wheelbarrow. All Mike's expensive artwork. If she had been tempted, and taken say a million pound daub, maybe she'd have to kill him to keep it.

Such treacherous thoughts, between chat about clouds and the likelihood of seeing any Orionids.

Chapter 29

The doorbell rang. Mia looked up from her laptop, and wished her dad had an answerphone. It was most likely Penny at the front door. Much easier to deal with her over an answerphone than have to go to the door and face her.

But no choice.

She went downstairs and opened the front door. She was right. Penny was there, wearing a purple jacket with matching lipstick. Looked fresh, maybe put on before she got out of her car. And perfume. Definitely not for Mia. She had a light brown handbag with a long strap over her shoulder, purple nails, leather thigh-length boots.

Dressed to kill.

Penny smiled brightly.

'Is your dad in?'

'I am sorry,' said Mia. 'You have just missed him. He's gone to price up a job in Seven Kings.' Then a thought. She could do some questioning herself. She didn't have to be the one stuck in the office all day staring at a screen. 'Would you like a cup of tea?'

'That would be very nice.'

Penny came in, her expression a grimace of disappointment. She hadn't come here to have tea with Mia. She followed Mia through the inner door, up the stairs to Jack's place. Her scent irritated Mia's nose, it was all she could do to stifle a sneeze. All that artificial stuff. She despised puffs and creams, and rarely wore makeup. As for leather boots, don't get her started on the crimes against animals.

Once in the flat, they went into the kitchen, where Mia put the kettle on. The room was presentable, more or less.

Jack had mostly washed up, just a few items left on the redundant dishwasher.

'Do you think he'll be back soon?' said Penny.

'No,' said Mia firmly, as she got mugs and the teapot ready. 'He said it was a big job with a tricky client who will try to cut his price to the bone.'

Penny shrugged. 'Ah well, can't be helped. He has to make a living.'

Mia poured the hot water into the teapot.

'What school are you at, Mia?'

Mia stifled rolling her eyes. The questions people ask when they don't know what to say.

'I've left,' she said. 'What's the point going to school when climate change is going to destroy us?'

Penny raised her eyebrows. 'That bad?'

'You came here by car without even thinking about the exhaust gases, I bet.' She almost added so did Nova and then drove off with Jack in his gas guzzler.

Cars everywhere. How can we possibly survive.

She had to get off this track. It would simply make her miserable, but almost everywhere she looked were signs of climate change, and people who took no responsibility. But Mia hadn't invited Penny up to put her on the spot over climate change. Guilty as she was. Everyone was.

'A car is so convenient,' said Penny.

She had heard that expression way too often. Applied to flying and to single use plastics. What an ugly word.

As convenient as a coffin was her usual rejoinder, but she withheld the phrase. Instead saying:

'Who do you think did it?'

Mia poured tea into the mugs, awaiting the answer, put out a jug of oat milk and a plate of biscuits. She was her mother's daughter as well as Jack's.

'Did what?'

Mia refrained from rolling her eyes.

'The murder, of course.'

'Do you know all about it?'

'I am involved in the investigation,' she said.

'What investigation?' said Penny sharply.

Mia was aware, she had said too much. This was all too new. What to say to whom when. How to impress without letting the cat out of the bag.

'Client confidentiality,' she said. The age old shut down, the go away phrase.

'Has your father been investigating?'

Oh, that perfume. She struggled to hold back a sneeze.

'Client confidentiality,' she repeated, grabbing a piece of kitchen roll, and squeezing her nose.

Penny stood up, hoisting her bag strap on her shoulder. 'I see you are going to say that all night. It's very irritating, so I won't stay for tea. Sorry to have put you to the effort.'

'I don't mean to be rude,' said Mia plaintively. 'It's just...'

Just she wasn't a practised liar, or a schmoozer. Her mum's word. But you can't just schmooze everyone into liking you. You have to say what you mean some of the time.

Penny had left the kitchen, not interested in Mia's excuses, and was already in the sitting room, where she halted, and looked around.

'His telescope isn't here,' she said. She turned on Mia. 'You lied to me. He has gone over Wanstead Flats.'

Mia was flummoxed. She'd either get her dad or herself in trouble.

'I'll go over the Flats and find him,' said Penny, heading for the flat door.

Mia was in a fix. Now what?

'I'll come with,' she said, grabbing her coat and woolly hat.

Penny stared at her quizzically.

'It's not safe on the Flats this time of night,' said Mia, adding, 'I know where he goes.'

'Let's go then,' said Penny. 'Intrepid investigator.'

Chapter 30

Jack pushed the wheelbarrow across the Flats with the telescope in its belly, Nova carried the mount over her shoulder. The night was enclosing them in autumn chilliness. Jack had a torch in his backpack but had no need for it, though it was very dark. The only light was from distant traffic and street lights on the rim of the Flats.

He and Nova were heading across football pitches, sticky with mud. Both of them wore boots, knowing what they were in for. He had on his work boots, she the ones she had bought for the walking group, paid for her by the police as it was part of her undercover role. Corruption, he'd called it, on our taxes, only half joking when she'd told him the price of the boots. Nova had corrected him; she was not simply an 'art chic' but a keen walker too, in her role. And the tax would be returned one hundredfold when they called in the stolen art.

Though, had she collared a piece? Who would know now that Mike was no longer around?

Surely not. A crooked cop, Nova? But the job tempts cops, all that wealth, and so easy to get a piece of the action. An old old story. Let it lie. Stick to the stars and the wonders of the night sky.

Jack could have walked to the spot blindfolded, having done it so often. With Mia, with Nova, but not for a while with her, as she'd been otherwise engaged.

'As I was undercover,' she said, walking alongside him, 'being Mike's girlfriend, I couldn't suggest me and you get back together. Could I?'

Jack smiled, unseen. 'Your motive for killing him.'

She nudged him in the ribs.

'Having done it once,' she said, 'it's much easier the second time round.'

'How clever of you to entice me out on the Flats to do your dirty work.'

'Clever?' she harrumphed. 'All I had to do was suggest it and you jumped at it.'

The dome of sky was deep purple, almost black. There was a copse of trees to their left, about a hundred yards away, but it had merged into the gloom as if wiped away.

'It was the company that decided me,' he said. 'I've missed you.'

True, in spite of his traitorous ramblings.

'If I'd had to listen once more to Mike Rayner telling me how brilliant he was, I could so easily have done him in myself.'

'Two motives then.' Adding lightly, 'you could have stolen a couple of his priceless stolen paintings?'

'How would I sell them?'

'You must know a dodgy fence or two.'

She harrumphed. 'Who would blackmail me for life.'

He couldn't detect any discomfort in this light chat on stolen artwork. And fair enough, how would she, a cop, sell them on?

'Stop a moment,' she said. He halted the wheelbarrow, she put down the mount, wriggling her shoulders. 'You always go so far on the Flats, Jack.'

'Got to get as far as we can from the light pollution.' He swung about, pointing out the ring of light surrounding the Flats. 'All those cars, street lights, houses, washing out the stars.'

'You don't have to convince me.'

'It's why I invited you.'

He pecked her on the cheek.

'Excuse me,' she said. 'it was me invited you.'

They were on the move again. There might be a few others on the Flats, a lone dog walker, a runner, like unseen ghosts. But here and now, it felt like the space was theirs utterly.

The night was chilly, a slight breeze, but no matter. They were dressed for it.

'A lot of cloud,' she said, looking at the heavens and the horizon.

'That's what I was thinking.'

In a few minutes, they had reached the site, a flat, grassed area in the centre of the Flats, on the edge of one of many footballs pitches. Always best to keep off them. The pitches got so churned up this time of year, you could slip and slide, and more importantly so could the mount and its precious cargo.

They began setting up. First the mount, getting it steady on its three legs, and level with the built in spirit level.

'Is it worth putting on the scope?' he said, with the instrument clutched to his chest. 'There's so much cloud. We'd never see Mars. And there's no moon tonight.'

'Leave the scope,' she said. 'Let's go for the Orionids. Way over to the south east.' She pointed that way.

He put the telescope back in the wheelbarrow, wrapping it in its blanket, like a cosseted baby. Their eyes were getting dark adapted, and would be more or less fully so in about 20 minutes. She took his hand, both were wearing fingerless gloves, their tips touching. He hadn't spotted before, but she was wearing sunglasses, a seeming oddity in the darkness. But he knew they got your eyes dark adapted more quickly.

She took them off. Jack was pleased that she knew as much as he did, and was as keen to be out under the night sky. He had missed her.

'I think that's Beetlejuice,' she said. The vulgarisation of Betelgeuse, the super red giant, always highest in the sky in the constellation Orion.

'If it were at the centre of the solar system,' he said, 'in place of the sun, it would swallow up Mercury, Venus, Earth, and Mars and most of the asteroid belt.'

'Show off. You are nearly as bad as Mike.'

'I'd better watch myself,' he said. 'I read it up just before we came out. Got to keep up with you. And let me say, before I forget my party piece, Betelgeuse is due to blow up. That is, in about one hundred thousand years, in a great supernova explosion which will be as bright as the half moon.'

'Not tonight then. Just as well, as we wouldn't see a single Orionid.'

'There's one!' he exclaimed. 'See.' He pointed out the glimmer of light that came out of the dark, like the flash of a white hot needle. 'Gone.'

'Missed it.'

'Let's have tea while we watch.'

'There's one!' she exclaimed.

Jack put out the camping stools that were in the wheelbarrow with the telescope, and took the thermos out of his backpack with its two cups.

'My contribution is a mushroom and sundried tomato pizza,' she said, taking the box out of her backpack. 'It's stone-baked and veggie, just in case Mia joined us.'

His daughter was hopefully heading off Penny, thought Jack, wondering how the professor would cope out here.

Chapter 31

Mia and Penny were heading for the Flats in Penny's car. Some classical music was playing, the sort of thing her mum liked.

Penny said, 'I saw some Spanish on your laptop.' It had been on the sitting room table. Mia had been searching for info on Liz's daughter.

'Got to to keep up,' Mia said. 'Or you forget.'

'I am glad you are not neglecting your studies.'

Patronising cow.

'Who do you think killed him?' Penny added.

'Me?' surprised to be asked.

'I don't see anyone else present.'

A sarky one, the way it was with teachers, as she knew from school and her mother. And professors too.

'One of the walkers did it,' she said.

Penny gave a short laugh. 'That's hardly giving anything away.'

They were silent a while, heading down Woodgrange High Street towards the Flats.

Penny said, 'Don't you find it rather risky being here with me? There's a one in seven chance I could be the killer.'

'I'd put it down to one in five,' said Mia, wondering even as she said the odds. She'd ruled out her dad and Nova. Though she was iffy about Nova. Cops can be dodgy, they can lie, plant evidence, and fill their pockets if the chance comes.

'One in five strikes me as a high risk, Mia. Worse than Russian roulette.'

Mia shrugged. 'Why would you kill me, if you are the killer? What do I know?'

'I can't think why.' Then added, 'Who does your father think did it?'

'He doesn't know yet. Dad gathers all the info together. Motives and such like, and he's all in the dark. And he can't sleep, he eats and drinks it. He's so obsessive. And then jumps up in the middle of the night with his Aha! triumph.'

They were approaching the Flats, near the tower block at the corner.

'Where does your dad park his van?'

'In the car park down Centre Road.'

Penny did a sharp right into Capel Road.

'I said the car park on Centre Road, not down here.'

'I don't believe you.'

Penny had slowed up, to not be too bumpy with the sleeping policemen on the roadway. On one side of the road were houses, on the other trees and shrubs fringing the Flats.

Mia looked at her as she concentrated on her driving. Why was she so intent on finding her father? What went on in her mathematical brain? Did she fancy him that much? The perfume was getting to her again. She squeezed her nose and closed her eyes. It was so sharp.

'There we are!' called out Penny.

Mia opened her eyes, just as they were passing her father's *Jack of All Trades* van. Couldn't be missed with that tag line on the sides.

'Where can we park?' mused Penny. 'There. I think I can just squeeze in.'

She parked the car a short way up the road, and they alighted. Mia was almost suitably dressed with her anorak, scarf and woolly hat, gloves in her pocket. She had on her trainers, not the best footwear, as it was boot terrain, but OK, even if her feet might get wet. Penny though was dressed for some other scenario, with her light jacket, heavy perfume and thigh length boots with their four inch heels.

'I wouldn't go over the Flats in those boots,' said Mia.

'I wouldn't normally,' said Penny, 'but let's live dangerously.'

More fool you, thought Mia, showing that professors could be as dumb as anyone.

Penny headed through a gap in the trees onto the Flats. She stopped as Mia caught up.

'Which way?'

'That way,' pointed Mia.

'Then we go the other way.'

And she set off. The wrong way, as Mia had anticipated her disbelief. Penny was slipping in those dreadful boots, made from dead animal skins. Serves her right.

'How far?' said Penny.

'Not far.'

Though how far was far? Not far for her in her trainers, anorak and gloves, but too far for Penny in those poncy boots.

Penny stopped, scanning around her.

'This is stupid. I'm getting covered in mud. Doesn't he have a light?'

'No,' said Mia. 'It would ruin the seeing.' A truth for a change. 'Only a hundred yards or so to go.'

'So' was elastic as 'far'.

Penny skidded on, mostly keeping to her feet, getting to the point where her goal might be closer than her car. Or might not be. As she was relying on a proven liar.

Mia took her across bumpy ground, an underground city of busy moles. She knew exactly where she was, and where her dad was too. Way over in the other direction.

'Do you want a hand?' said Mia, seeing her stumble.

'I can manage,' said Penny, scrambling along, arms flailing to keep her balance. She would not request help from a teenager.

'Why does he have to come out so far?'

'To get away from light pollution,' said Mia. 'You should know that. And you shouldn't wear those dead animal boots.'

'What a prig you are!'

'I've been called worse. By the fuzz.'

They walked on in silence across the bumpy grass and moss, less than shadows in the darkness.

Penny suddenly cried out. Mia who was a stride or two ahead, turned around.

'I've sprained my ankle. Oh God!'

Mia got out her phone and shone it. Penny was seated on the wet ground massaging her left ankle and moaning.

Now what?

It was Penny's choice to go in this direction, to go across the Flats at all. Mia had told her not to. But then Mia had deliberately taken her over rough ground, where in the dark, with those heels, an accident was no surprise.

Penny could have said no. She could have turned back. She was a professor.

Too late for any discussion of the rights and wrongs.

'I'll phone Dad,' she said.

Mia pressed his number. Her phone rang on. And then went to voicemail.

'His phone is off,' said Mia. 'He doesn't like to be disturbed when out stargazing.'

'What am I going to do? I can't walk.'

There weren't many options.

'I'll go get him,' said Mia. 'Give me your number.'

They swapped phone numbers.

'Have my hat and scarf,' said Mia. And put her woolly hat on Penny's head, down over her ears, and the scarf round her neck. Her own hair was long and wild enough to almost be as good as a beanie. 'And my gloves.'

She handed them over and headed off into the darkness.

Chapter 32

Nova and Jack were eating pizza, drinking tea and watching the occasional shooting star. Mars was somewhere covered in cloud. Forget it. The weather gods had it in for British astronomers. The wind had picked up. They sat in the dark, knees touching.

She said, 'Who do you think did it? Any clearer?'

He didn't need clarity on the 'it'. Jack had asked the question himself in the same form of words. The big who.

'I know I didn't,' he said. 'So that's down to six. I really don't want it to be you. I couldn't wait 20 years for you to be released.'

'Some lover you are.'

'For the sake of a peaceful life, let's call it five. They all have motives.' He went through them on his fingers. 'Phil is resentful that Mike wouldn't take any more of his pictures. Liz, there's something with the daughter in Spain, I don't know what yet. With Deneb it's racism, Mike hated him...'

'Wouldn't it be more like Mike would kill him?'

Jack knew there was more to it for Deneb, but was giving no hints.

'Fiona is somehow mixed up in Mike's art dealing. She's shacked up with George Taplow who happens to be Penny's ex husband...'

'Sounds like musical chairs. There's one!'

'Blink and you miss 'em. More tea?'

'Yeh.'

She put the cup close enough so he could see it and he topped it up. A little warmth left in the liquid.

'As for Penny, well, she had a brief scene with Mike and I don't think it went well.'

'There's one, and another! Two in a row, wow!'

'Won't get another for five minutes. No. There's one!'

'Suppose it wasn't one of the walkers,' she said.

'You mean someone waiting by the Witch's Tree? How would they know he'd be there on his own?'

'Might just be lucky,' she said. 'Whoever it was came to kill him, was going to stay ahead of the group, he or she knew the route, and there is Mike, what luck, on his own by the Witch's Tree. Not a chance to be missed.'

'Possible. Just about. There's one!'

She tugged at his arm.

'Is someone calling? Listen.'

In the distance Jack could just pick up a voice.

'Dad! Dad!'

He stood up, put on his phone light to make himself visible and waved his arms.

'It's Mia,' he said to Nova. 'What's she doing here?' He continued waving his arms. 'Here! Here!'

They saw the glimmer of her phone, not her body as yet. Jack ran out to greet her.

She coming in, he going her way. they came together. Mia was breathless, bending over, barely able to speak.

'You OK?' he said. 'What's going on?'

'I'm fine. Just out of breath. It's Penny...' Hands on his hips, she inhaled vigorously. 'Sprained her ankle. She's out there.' And pointed vaguely across the Flats.

Nova had joined them.

'Better get packed up,' she said, having got the gist of it.

They led Mia back to their area, sat her on a stool, and gave her a mug of tea, a little warmth for her cold hands. The scope was already in the wheelbarrow wrapped it in its blanket, as there had been too much cloud to warrant setting it up. Nova gathered up the mount.

The other bits and pieces were gathered in: stools, thermos, pizza box, cups.

'Lead on,' said Jack. 'You don't have to run. We can walk quickly. You don't die of a sprained ankle.'

They set off.

'Can you call her, Dad?'

'Sure. Take the wheelbarrow.'

Mia took over. Jack pressed her number on his phone. 'Penny?'

'I'm here, Jack.'

'You alright?'

'Cold, shivering,' she said. 'My ankle is hurting like crazy, might be a broken bone. It's awfully swollen. Can't walk. Just had a go, too painful.'

Mia called into the phone, 'Be there in five minutes, Penny.'

They trundled on.

Chapter 33

As they pushed on, Jack said, 'What was she doing here in the first place?'

'She came to see you,' said Mia. 'She came upstairs, and saw the scope had gone. Knew you had gone over the Flats.'

'So why is she way over that way?' He could guess why, as Mia knew the Flats, knew where he set his telescope up. He wanted her to confirm her trickery.

'Why do you think?' said Mia, somewhat annoyed. 'I was trying to save you from a big scene. And now look what I've done!'

'What do you mean?'

They were crossing the football pitches, Mia directing them. There was little to see in the gloom, beyond the far off lights. No person, no bird, the ground sloshy underfoot.

'She's dressed for the catwalk,' exclaimed Mia. 'Thin short coat, perfume like a whorehouse...'

'What do you know of whorehouses?' he said.

'I'm just telling you. In her car, the pong was stinging my nose like needles. And those boots! You should see her boots. Thigh length with four inch heels. I told her she was crazy to go out onto the Flats.'

'With you leading her astray,' said Nova. 'Sure.'

'I pointed her in your direction, but she didn't believe me.'

'I wonder why,' said Jack.

Mia laughed. 'She was doing the opposite of what I told her. So I double bluffed.' She stopped. 'It's my fault. I shouldn't have taken her over those mole hills.'

'Take the wheelbarrow.'

Mia did so. Jack phoned.

'You OK, Penny?'

'Cold as an icebox. I'm sure I have a broken bone.'

'We'll take you straight to hospital. Be there very soon.'

'My phone is running out of juice, Jack,' said Penny. 'Been using the light. Just 2% left. Better switch it off. Don't hang about. I'm an icicle.'

She hung up.

'She's freezing,' he told Mia and Nova, 'and thinks she's broken a bone.'

Jack took over the wheelbarrow, thinking he should have texted her earlier that day, to stop her coming to see him tonight. Not hand over excuses to Mia. Then again, if you wear four inch heels and come over the Flats with the ground soggy as rice pudding... Not that Mia needed to have led her over molehills in the dark.

She, Mia and himself. Apportion the blame.

Nova said, 'I'm surprised at her getting into this mess. Penny is in a walking group. She knows not to go over wet ground in unsuitable footwear. Why would she do that?'

'Love shmuv,' muttered Mia. One of her mother's phrases.

They had come to the area of molehills.

'Somewhere round here,' said Mia.

Darkness overwhelmed the Flats, the glowering cloud threatening rain, and shrouding them in gloom. Black outlines on marginally less black background, like the black cat in a black room, somewhere around here, as Mia said.

'I'll phone her,' said Jack.

No reply. He tried several times. Each time, it went to voice mail. He left a message asking her to phone back, as they were nearby.

'She's out of battery,' he said. 'Let's be methodical. I've a torch in my bag.' He took off his backpack and searched about inside. 'Got it.' A large torch, with a long black handle and a big head. He turned it on, it shone red, needing the dimness when they were stargazing. Jack tore off the red film on the glass, and circled the bright beam across the area.

'Penny! Penny!' called Mia, her hands cupped round her mouth.

Nova joined in the calling while Jack swung around the light beam, carefully crossing the molehills. This would be treacherous in bad footwear, he thought. And badly dressed too. Maybe she had passed out. Perhaps worst than a broken bone. Internal bleeding, who knows?

They separated, crossed and recrossed the area, shouting, shining the torch and their phones.

After about ten minutes, they came together, frustrated. Mia was getting cold. Jack had given her his gloves, Nova her woolly hat.

'I shouldn't have left her,' Mia exclaimed. 'But your phone wasn't on. I didn't have any choice.'

'Don't blame yourself,' said Nova.

'Can she have crawled off somewhere?' said Mia. 'Into those trees, maybe.'

'I don't think so,' said Jack. 'You don't crawl far with a broken bone. And she knew we were on the way.'

'She's been kidnapped!' exclaimed Mia. 'Penny knows something important and was coming to tell you. But he got to her first. The murderer is a serial killer, Dad. And it was me who left her.'

Jack put a hand on her shoulder.

'Let's go to the van,' he said.

Mia was reluctant, wanting to keep searching, but Jack persuaded her. They had been over the area too many times.

'Kidnapped! I am sure of it!'

They trudged over the wet turf to the edge of the Flats. The wind had blown the cloud in, so might clear later when it blew it out again, but all thoughts of stargazing had gone. Those brief glimmers, he and Nova had so enjoyed, particles the size of sand grains shooting into the atmosphere at an immense speed and burning up in a flash. Gone.

Joy burnt up.

Jack had taken the mount from Nova and slung it over his shoulder, while she'd taken over the wheelbarrow. Mia had the torch and was spraying the beam over the sward, as if Penny might be lying out there comatose, or crawling towards them like a wounded soldier on a battlefield.

At the edge of the Flats, Nova tipped the wheelbarrow into the roadway. The van was about 30 yards further up. They went along to it. Jack opened up and they stowed the gear in as well as the wheelbarrow. The van was his toolshed as wall as his transport.

'Where's her car?' said Nova.

It struck them all at once, the suspicion. They followed Mia up the road as she headed for it.

Mia stood by a space along the kerb.

'It was here,' she exclaimed. 'I remember the porch of that house.'

'Kidnapped with her own car, do you think?' said Jack, who didn't believe that at all.

'She's having a laugh,' exclaimed Mia. 'She didn't sprain her ankle, didn't break a bone or anything at all!'

'I was about to call the police,' said Nova.

'She's got my hat, gloves and scarf!'

Jack was half amused, half annoyed at their fruitless search on the Flats, at losing time with Nova and the meteor shower. But on reflection, who would say he hadn't deserved it?

They drove back to Jack's.

Once in the flat, Jack tried phoning Penny. No reply. He texted her. Quite useless as it depended on her replying. Mia told him that it could be the kidnappers replying. She had reverted to her wild idea. Or was it so wild?

'I am still worried,' said Nova. 'We need to know that she is safe. Have you got her home address?'

Jack searched it out, among the papers on the table and gave it to her.

Nova phoned the local police station.

'This is DC Nova Taylor. I am concerned about the safety of Penny Hicks. She may be badly hurt. Can you send a car round to her house and call me back.' She gave the address. 'As soon as possible, please.'

They had tea and toast. A little glumly, as there was the smidgeon of uncertainty. Mia being certain the kidnapper had taken her in her car. And was blaming herself for leaving Penny helpless. Jack was telling her it was unlikely. But he couldn't rule it out.

The phone call came.

Nova spoke to the officer who had called at the house. Penny had come to the door, bright as a sparkler, no broken bones or any sign of a sprain.

Mystery mostly revealed, they sat at the table, drinking tea. A trick. Not a kidnapper in sight.

'Why do all that?' said Jack. 'Get us chasing our tails half the night.'

Nova shook her head and chuckled.

'I get it totally. Penny suspected you were up to no good,' she said.

'She knew you were two-timing,' said Mia.

Jack nodded, uncomfortable at his daughter's inference, true as it might be.

'You stood her up,' said Nova. 'In her mind anyway. She wasn't going to be humiliated, so turned the tables well and truly.'

Chapter 34

Mia was up first in the morning. She quickly had breakfast, saying she needed to get to the shop where they were working. Jack didn't ask her why, but hoped that she was getting somewhere with her Spanish investigations concerning Liz's daughter. He gave her the shop keys, and she left. He would join her in half an hour or so.

Nova had left last night, once she had ascertained that Penny was OK. She, the cop, had had to clear up the uncertainty, as, if anything untoward had happened, she'd have taken the flak. For being on the spot and for not taking appropriate action.

For breakfast, Jack had muesli and a banana. That's what you get when Mia shops. No bacon, no eggs, and oat milk to go in tea. He could never save the planet as he ate the wrong things, given a choice that is, and drove a gas guzzler. Mia said the government had to make people go green. But who would vote for such a government?

Not easy answers, as he spooned his muesli, to our reluctance to save ourselves. Like badly brought up kids, we have all the wrong habits. Mia was slowly getting through to him, but if other people were as bad as he was, then we are doomed.

Mia had chastised him for saying that. Say it and you give up the fight with a clear conscience. March, demonstrate, demand a cleaner, cooler planet.

Before it is too late.

Not doomed then. Nearly doomed.

Enjoy your muesli.

He thought of Nova, Their hour watching the shooting stars. They had got close again and might have got closer, if not interrupted by the Penny episode.

She had lied, so convincingly, saying how cold she was, that she might have broken a bone. Probably speaking to him, all along, from the warmth of her car.

Why had she done it?

Mia had lied to her about where he was. So lies of revenge maybe. Penny had come over, dressed to the nines. To seduce him, was that so, or male ego wanting it that way? Or, more likely, to get him on her side for whatever reason, and when she realised that wasn't going to happen, sending them all off on a wild goose chase, calling across the Flats, by torchlight and by phone, worried that she was lying in the mud, unconscious. Mia, especially upset.

A woman not to be crossed.

He rose. The washing up could be left till he came back after work. Jack set off for the shop. Today, he must get some work done. He couldn't just be a detective. With just one client, it was a joke.

Jack walked to the shop. It was only ten minutes away. Along his road, the plane trees were losing their leaves, many on the pavement like dead flatfish. The sky was low and brooding, it was drizzling. He put his hood up, he wasn't an umbrella person. So you get a bit wet, he would say.

You could get very wet for the sake of image.

Jack opened the shop door and walked into a storm. Music was blaring from the back office and three young people, a boy and two girls, one of whom was Mia, were on the floor, with a bundle of sticks, and a heap of placards with slogans on. With staple guns, they were making up banners, by sticking sticks to the placards. Preparing for a climate change demo.

Youngsters out to confound the doomsayers. Beat them over the head with banners, if nothing else.

Above them stood Mrs Elks like a Fury, ranting at them. It was hard to hear her over the music coming from the office, but the young people were ignoring her. Deliberately, as you couldn't ignore her. Or rather, Jack never had.

She immediately turned on Jack, yelling at him.

'You are in charge here! What is the meaning of this?'

Mrs Elks wore a dark brown, captain's peaked hat, as if she were the master of the ship, any ship she was sailing on. Her large red umbrella was folded by the door.

'They are making banners,' he had to yell into her ear.

'This is not your space,' she yelled back.

'I'll get them to pack up.' He bent down to Mia. 'Can you pack up now?'

'Sure,' said Mia, and transmitted it to her friends. Willing to hear from him, but not from the moose.

They began bundling the banners together and taking them into the back room.

'I can't hear myself think,' declared Mrs Elks, pressing her hands to her ears.

She had on a long brown dress, almost to her ankles and a yellow waistcoat, open at the front. She was always so stylish, and he'd hoped at the beginning that style came with pleasantness. But found quickly, there was no connection.

Mrs Elks watched the youngsters taking the banners into the office.

'I can't have political banners here!' she exclaimed. 'Not in my shop.'

'Climate change isn't political,' he said. Though he knew sometimes it was, sometimes it wasn't, depending who you were talking to. 'We all need to save the planet.'

'Not in my shop,' she repeated. She pointed to the office. 'Is that going to be a den of anarchists?'

'No, it's my agency,' he said. 'But for now, as I've hardly got going, they can keep their banners there.'

'This is preposterous. Music to bust your eardrums and, on top of it, political banners.'

'Climate change is not political.' He said it again, as clearly it annoyed her. He had been too nice to her. Mia saw that as ineffective, as clearly it was, Mrs Elks taking advantage of any niceness.

'I can't have you abusing my office,' she exclaimed, pointing it out as if he were unclear of where she meant.

'I only have it for a year,' he said. 'It's our deal.'

'You talked me into it,' she said, arms folded. An aggressive stance, though few of hers were otherwise.

It was not his take that he had talked her into anything. He had suggested having the office, and she had snapped it up. But that wasn't worth an argument.

'It's in the contract,' he said. He had it out of his back-pack in readiness.

'Ah, the contract, the contract, the one and only holy contract,' she fumed. 'It's time we renegotiated that stupid piece of paper.'

All the banners were in the office, sticks, placards and staple guns too. Mrs Elks strode over and slammed the door on the young radicals. The music could still be heard, but was less ear-splitting.

'You haven't done much since yesterday,' she said, looking around the shop at the counter frames.

He had of course left early to go and see Taplow (and Fiona), Liz too, but he was making no concessions.

'Good work takes time.'

She snorted, but it would be difficult for her to argue about piece rates for carpentry.

He said, 'If you are unhappy with the contract, I'll be willing to give up the office, if you agree to pay me the full price.'

'No, no.' She wagged a stern finger. 'That was far too high. You can have 70%. Take it or leave it.'

'Then I keep the office,' he said.

The office door opened. Mia came out with the kettle and went out to the back scullery to fill it. Mrs Elks strode over and slammed the office door.

'To be an anarchists' den? No, no. Never.'

'It will be a detective agency. In a few weeks. When we have completed our advertising campaign.'

Mumbo jumbo, what advertising campaign, but let her prove otherwise.

'Seventy-five per cent. My final offer.'

Two final offers, he noted, one after another. Anger doesn't make for good deals.

'If you agree a contract,' he said, 'then you should stick to it. That's the whole point of contracts.'

He waved the paper at her. It was all he had, but she had signed it. Bluster as much as she liked, there was her signature.

'I shall talk to my husband.'

She gathered up her umbrella and was out the door.

It was not likely she'd be straight back, as she liked a strong exit. He watched her walk away, her umbrella up to keep the rain off her outfit. Jack went to the back office, put his head inside. In spite of the cramped space, they were working on the banners.

Mia returned with the kettle.

'How's the moose,' she said.

'She's offered me 75% of the original contract to vacate the office. I said I want 100% or we stay. I would accept 90%, we can't work here with her complaining all day. But I'll have to push her. So you have my permission to be a nuisance every morning until she gets nearer to my terms. But now she's gone, please turn the music down.'

'Oh, that's just for her. A van is coming in two hours to pick up the banners. Can we work in the shop?'

'OK. But by the window. I'm going to be sawing, so keep away from where I'm working.'

The second counter frame needed completing, all the pieces to be screwed in place. Before starting, he moved the first counter frame, so it was a barrier to the banner crew, as he'd be creating a lot of sawdust and working with a powerful blade.

It was a companionable time. They had switched the radio to 6 Music. Radio 1 was for kids, Mia had told him, top twenty crap played over and over. They made tea, joked, called him Mr Bell a couple of times, until he insisted on Jack. Then they didn't call him anything, not wanting to use a first name for someone the age of their parents.

On completing the second counter frame, he checked it for firmness. Sturdy, as it was meant to be. If he wanted to push Mrs Elks into a better deal, his work had to be good, though she would moan anyway, whatever he did, her tactic for chipping away at the price tag.

The next stage was putting on the sides and the counter tops. The wood was stacked against the wall, where it had waited plaintively for the last few days.

Jack went into the office and phoned Penny.

She answered after just a few rings, unlike the tail end of last night, when they'd been searching for her fruitlessly, and all messages to her had gone to answerphone.

'Good morning, Jack.' A bright greeting.

'No broken bones?' he queried.

'I'm fine,' she said. 'No thanks to your lying daughter.'

'You managed a few fibs yourself.'

'She led me over hill and dale.'

'There are no hills on the Flats.' He chuckled. 'Or are you talking about molehills?'

'Simply a metaphor.'

'You were unsuitably dressed. Why did you come?'

She was silent for a few seconds.

'To see you. How was I to know you'd be out on the Flats?'

'But once you knew. Those boots...'

'Nearly ruined. One hundred and seventy pounds, less one penny.'

'I'm not worth it,' he said.

'You are most surely not. The odd penny perhaps, though that's pushing it.'

Mia came in, seeing he was on the phone, mimed drinking tea. He gave her the thumbs up, and she left, closing the door.

'You led us on a dreadful chase, scrambling around those molehills,' he said. 'Mia was distraught. She thought you were badly hurt, kidnapped, heaven knows what.'

'She'll get over it.'

'Will I?'

'Tell me. I really don't know.'

He didn't know what to say to her. Nova was once again in the frame, but he didn't want to burn his boats with Penny, as he and Nova were so on and off. Great when it worked, other times there were quarrels to shout the house down. Penny's ruse had turned him off her, but overnight had turned him on again. The audacity of it.

'You were lying in the mud, with a broken bone, freezing...' he said.

'I was in my car waiting for you to phone,' she corrected him, 'the heater on, listening to Scheherazade, Rimsky-Korsakov. It's such a beautiful symphony. I'll play it for you some time. Just the music to be icy cold to, dying on the Steppes, when your troika has thrown you. I had to turn it off when you phoned.'

'Sorry to have disturbed you.'

'Yes, it was an interruption. I lost the rapture, of warmth and music, playing the distressed female. But needs must.' She stopped for a second, then said, 'Were you with Nova?'

'On my own,' he lied, 'till Mia came.'

'So why was she lying?'

'You'll have to ask her. Though she has a thing against teachers.'

'I'm a professor!'

'Not in those shoes, you weren't.' He laughed. 'I suppose it's tit for tat.'

'You don't hate me?'

'I did last night, when we got the message from the cops that you were fine. I'd have cheerfully fed you to the lions.'

'And this morning?'

'Less cheerfully.'

She laughed. 'I have to go, Jack. I'd like to talk more, but I'm giving a lecture to third years, and I have to be on my toes, there's some bright bods amongst the dross. We must meet soon. Very soon. Tomorrow perhaps. There's lots I have to say to you.'

She ended the call. He went back to work. Sawing, and trying to fit her words into his worldview. Was she flirting? She didn't know he'd been with Nova. But why would she?

It was not as if they had found her.

Mid morning, the banners and two of the campaigners left. A van, very like his own, had come and the three had loaded up.

Such vans, it seemed, were OK for demos. Not for swanning around in, as Mia put it.

'The banners are for Saturday,' said Mia, as the van left, 'At London City Airport. Against internal flights. The most polluting per mile. Now I'm off to Spain. Hasta la vista.'

She took the radio and went into the office.

It took him a second to understand. And then he recalled. Liz's daughter in Barcelona, some possible complication there.

He had the space to himself. Banner crew gone, he could think again. Murder and sex. He hoped AI would never get into mind reading, and all be revealed. Love, hate, and lies. His thoughts drifted as he marked up and sawed. He had no leverage in their meandering. Murder and sex.

That ruse of Penny's last night, it had so hurt at the time, all that searching in the dark, but in retrospect, the cheek of it, so sexy.

Chapter 35

At lunch break, Jack walked over to Forest Gate Police Station. It was only quarter of a mile away. DI Fayyad Kamani was in and had agreed to see him.

At the station, once the desk officer had checked Jack's appointment, he was taken to Fayyad's office. Quite a small room, he'd thought a detective inspector would have more footage. Space here is at a premium, Fayyad had told him. I'm lucky to get a separate office at all.

They shook hands. Fayyad was as smartly dressed as always. Seven suits he wore in rotation, one taken daily to the cleaners, with another taken out. He disliked wearing the same suit twice as he had to do at conferences when he had to stay overnight. 'Stay smart, and you think smart,' he had said. But he allowed Jack as an exception. The one that proved the rule.

Wonky reasoning, thought Jack. Hedge fund managers and con men wore suits, but he kept his counsel. Fayyad was a good friend, so why argue over the way he was and would forever be?

'What can I do for you, Jack?'

They were seated either side of the desk, behind him a shelf with a photo of his wife and two children, growing teenagers, next to it, a silver cricket cup for the Met Police league. On the other side, a team photo, members in their cricket whites, Fayyad in the centre holding the bat.

'I'm investigating Mike Rayner's murder for a client,' said Jack.

'Client?' queried Fayyad. 'Is this competition?'

Jack smiled at his friend's joshing. They had been mates since their days at Cumberland school.

'You have far more resources than I have,' he said. 'But I need some help and it might assist you too.'

'Tell me.'

'I need to know if George Taplow has an alibi for the murder.'

Fayyad didn't know who Taplow was. So Jack filled him in. An art dealer, ex-husband of Penny Hicks, and now shacking up with Fiona Jones, both women on the walk.

Nova could have told Fayyad that, but she was off the case, and clearly hadn't passed on that bit of info to her boss. Suspicious or just slipped her mind?

'You have been getting around, Jack,' said Fayyad, obviously impressed, as this was an avenue they hadn't looked into. Jack gave him Taplow's contact details.

'I'll set that in motion, Jack. Anything else?'

'Have you had a metal detector run over the crime scene?'

'Not that I know of.'

'I think you'll find the knife, if you do.'

'Can you tell me why?'

'Not as yet, as you may not find it, but if you do, can you contact me as soon as.'

'Fair deal. You will swap any further info you get?'

Jack said he would, as what else could he say, but it wasn't entirely honest, as Fayyad no doubt knew. Jack had a client and there were secrets he could not disclose.

He rose, saying, he must get back to work, work that earned him money, rather than crime solving that earned him peanuts.

Fayyad asked him where he was working in case he needed to call in. Jack gave him the address, and then left the office, accompanied by Fayyad. It was strict policy to accompany visitors to the civvy side of the counter.

In the hallway, heading towards the foyer, Nova came out of a side room. She was smartly dressed in a navy dress suit, befitting Fayyad's assistant. Though, she was not on his current case, being too involved as a participant on the walk, as well as undercover. Too many complications for her to be on the murder team.

'Hello, Jack.'

Friendliness, not affection. Expected in her work setting.

'Hello, Nova. Having a good day?'

'Boring,' she said. 'Paperwork up to my eyeballs. I envy you private eyes.'

Except when it comes to wages, thought Jack.

A few more pleasantries, and they parted. With Fayyad by his side, no intimacy was possible. Jack and Fayyad shook hands in the foyer, promising to keep in touch on the case.

On the way back to the shop, he popped into the Romford Road McDonald's and bought two hamburgers. The first meat for three days. He wouldn't go into the shop with it, steaming and slopped in sauce. Mia would complain for a week about dead animals and McDonald's employment policies.

Jack went into the Emmanuel churchyard, convenient, as it was on the way back. They had done it up recently, quite well paved, with new benches. Not bad work, as he looked it over, wondering who had done it. How they had got the money, churches always being short on cash.

The rain had stopped before he'd come out, though it was still clouded over, and might start again. But late October, that was to be expected, the clocks going back this weekend. Dark evenings for stargazing, the best of the year, when and if the clouds cleared.

Jack wiped the bench with one of the McDonald's tissues, sat himself down, and enjoyed the meat feast. Stretching out his legs, a little chilly, but not a bad spot, behind the church in a windbreak. He thought of the brief encounter with Nova at the police station. Work manners, but he detected her pleasure at seeing him.

Good old Fayyad.

He had always been a reliable mate, one you could call on when in trouble. And he'd had need to. And now Jack was going freelance, a more than useful contact. With luck, he'd get back to Jack quickly on Taplow and the efficacy of the metal detector. Things were fitting into place, brick by brick, a wall of sorts was building, but still somewhat shaky.

A permanent fixture, he hoped, not set for a Jenga collapse.

Jack finished the burgers. A good filler. He threw the evidence of his sins into the bin, and headed back. He'd have a cuppa to wash it down. His turn to make the tea.

Chapter 36

At the shop, Mia had bought them a baguette, hummus and tomatoes. He told her he'd eaten in the police canteen with Fayyad.

And made tea. Jack reckoned he was about three behind. But she'd been making for her demo mates too, so maybe they were quits. He wondered if that altercation in the morning could rebound. Mia and her pals, certainly, shouldn't have been making banners in the front shop. The loud music was not a problem, as that was expected of builders.

If Mrs Elks went to law, he'd find the banner making impossible to argue. He doubted she would, as lawyers cost money, and she fought over every penny. But you never knew.

'No more banner making,' he said to Mia.

She was at her laptop, eating lunch. He told her why.

'But they are coming back tomorrow,' she said.

'Call them off. Sorry. Annoy her for sure, but we don't want to give her cause to take us to court.'

Mia reluctantly agreed.

He got back to work.

Counter frames made, he marked up the wood for sides and for the counter tops. Could he and Nova make a go of it once more? The big question, coming, slipping away, then back centre stage again. The bugbear was her cancelling dates at the last minute. The option was never to go on dates, of course. No cinema, restaurants, no telescope sessions. Or rather, make them spontaneous. Even then, there was risk of interruption, the bane of the detective's life, in a restaurant once, their order just on the table, another time, while watching a film; the whole cinema cursing the cop rushing for the exit.

Professors were simpler. Or so, he assumed. His knowledge didn't go deep in the realms of academe. But he couldn't imagine Penny rushing off for an emergency lecture.

Jack put on his ear protectors and began sawing. Mia had bought the protectors for a birthday present, not that he'd appreciated them, as they were for the job, not for him. But the saw howled like a banshee, and builders were notoriously careless, needing pushing to ensure they wore the right gear. The mantra on the gates of the big firms was: No Boots, No Helmet. No Job. It was the little guys, the small firms, the individuals like him who thought it would never happen to them. No union to enforce health and safety.

He was better than he was. And more grateful for the ear protectors.

Mia came in while he was sawing one of the side pieces. She kept back, until he'd sawn to the end, then tapped him on the shoulder.

'Got it!' she exclaimed.

He couldn't hear Mia with the protectors on, sliding them round his neck, her excitement had him follow her into the office, where she showed him, on her laptop, a Spanish newspaper article. There was a photo of a young woman, late 20s or so, he'd say, in piece in Spanish, a language he didn't know. There had been the option as school but football was the only one he'd taken up.

'What does it say?'

'That's Gill Greene, and that's a Barcelona paper. A Spanish one, the Catalan papers I gave up on. Google Translate mangled them.'

'What does it say?' he repeated impatiently.

'It says, an English woman, Gill Greene, aged 29, was arrested for shoplifting, and the magistrate has ordered a psychiatric report.'

'Why?'

'She took a parrot. A green one. She said, it was her mother calling her. As if the parrot was a phone.'

'A troubled young lady.'

'Not so young.'

No point discussing perspectives on age. He was more than ten years past Gill Greene's age, while his daughter had more than that to go.

'Well done,' he said.

'Is it important?'

'Could be.'

'You always say that,' she snorted.

He had no other work for her. But she had the website to work on and ads to put out on social media. He left her, commending her work again. It was hard finding work for her. They needed clients. More than one.

How many could they handle? Wryly, he wondered, whether he would ever find out.

Jack was about to get back to sawing, when Fayyad rushed into the shop. He pulled him by the arm.

'Let's go,' he said.

'Where?'

'The Witch's Tree. They have found the knife.'

Jack told Mia to hold the fort. He grabbed his coat and set off with Fayyad, as Mia bolted the door on them.

The car was parked outside the shop. Jack got in and belted up. Fayyad attached the siren to the roof. Blues and twos on full as they set off, in ear-piercing blare and flashing lights, alerting the traffic as they headed along Woodgrange, zipping in and out of stopped cars. Jack knew their journey wasn't urgent, not if the knife had been found, just that Fayyad was busy. And enjoyed being seen to be.

Once hitting Centre Road, through the Flats, Fayyad turned off the siren. They were just another car on the road.

The sky was darkening, heavy with brooding, low cloud, utterly obvious across the Flats. Jack thought, it's going to come down in buckets any minute. Way across, near the horizon, he could see where it was already raining. Surely, heading this way at a pace.

'CSI were about to pack up,' said Fayyad, 'but we rushed a metal detector to them. Why they didn't have one in their kit, beats me. And within twenty minutes, they had found the knife. I was going over to see it and talk to the crime scene co-ordinator, your shop was on the way; I thought Jack would want to be in on this.'

'Thanks,' he said.

It had begun to rain, as they passed the car park on the Flats. Light rain, and then, as if a tap had been turned on full, it was belting down in darts, blown in by a fierce wind. Within a few seconds streams were rushing along the gutters. Lightning flashed, sparking into the horizon, the boom a few seconds later. Visibility shortened in the pelting mist. Fayyad had slowed up as cars passed, coming the other way, ploughing waves of water. The windscreen wipers were unable to keep up with the deluge.

They were enclosed, yet utterly exposed. A lightning flash struck a tree a hundred metres away, almost instantly followed by a boom of thunder.

'We are a sitting target,' exclaimed Fayyad. 'A box of metal. Let's get out of here!'

They had come to the roundabout at the end of the Flats, the rain was easing, as if a giant bucket had been poured over them, and all that was left were the drips.

Across the roundabout, up Blake Hall road, trees on either side, tennis courts, the golf course, and the deluge had become light rain. Blue was widening the cloud, like shutters being open on a sunny morning. A rainbow was growing in the north east, deepening as he watched, orange, yellow, blue, a hint of green, with the sun glinting on the wet tarmac ahead.

'Gave the car a good wash,' said Fayyad.

Jack doubted that any vehicle of Fayyad's needed it.

'Did you contact George Taplow?' he said.

'Yes, I did. Sent an officer round with one question. Where were you at 11 am on Saturday morning?' Fayyad laughed. 'He wasn't happy, picking on the first black man and all that, but was given the option answer now or come to the station as a suspect. So Taplow answered. Why be difficult, we don't want to bring him. This is a murder case, not kids pinching sweets from the Co-op. He said he was at an art auction in Hampstead, where he'd bought a couple of paintings. We are checking up on it.'

The car had turned into Bush Road, and, a hundred yards up, pulled off the road in a squelchy mud area overlooked by trees. The rain had stopped, the sun was shining, as if those few minutes before were a movie.

Fayyad put thin plastic protectors over his shoes, not to protect the crime scene but his shoes. He locked up and they headed up the trail.

The track was sloshy, big puddles in places, going from side to side of the trail, though the rain had stopped. Jack wasn't bothered by puddles in his work boots, or mud on his overalls, so what? But this was not Fayyad's terrain, he slowly picked his way through the puddles, mud splattering his trousers.

'Look at them,' he declared in exasperation. 'If I'd have known it was going to be like this, I'd not have come.'

It was only a few hundred yards up the track, but took all of ten minutes, with Jack stopping every so often for Fayyad to catch up. Fayyad knew the way, and kept directing Jack straight ahead, having come to the crime scene several times.

Two men in wellington boots and CSI gear came in view. They had their hoods down and were winding up crime scene tape. Jack got to them before Fayyad who was struggling along about thirty yards behind.

'You must have got clobbered in the storm,' he said.

'Man oh man, we were stuck in the open,' said one of the CSIs, a middle aged stocky man, balding. 'Like Noah's flood. Just as well we had this gear on. We were just about to take it off, but no way once it came hammering down. Only lasted a few minutes, but what a deluge.'

Fayyad had caught up.

'Nice mess you've got here, John,' he said to the man Jack had been talking to, indicating the puddly ground.

'Luckily, we are done,' he said.

'We've come to see the knife,' said Fayyad.

'Bring over the knife, Toby,' he called to his colleague.

Toby, a tall black man, was geared up like his partner. He went to a plastic box, near the tree, the Witch's Tree, with its roots exposed on the path side and a cavity underneath them, now full of muddy water. Taking the lid off the box, he took out a plastic bag containing the knife, and brought it over to Fayyad for appraisal.

'Nothing special,' said Fayyad, holding the bag, so Jack could see the contents. 'A long kitchen knife, probably from a set. Though it looks like it has been sharpened.'

'Could chop cabbage,' said Jack, 'into very small pieces. Where did you find it?

Toby said, 'I went over the ground with the metal detector.' He pointed it out the machine, leaning against the tree, two handles attached to the central upright with a flat plate at the bottom end. 'And I found the knife in there.' He pointed out a woody area. 'Can you see that metal pole, about ten yards in? There.'

Jack went for a closer look.

Coming back, he said, 'Whoever did the murder, got rid of the knife quickly.'

'Just stuck in the earth,' said Toby, 'vertical, a few inches down, leaves on the top. No chance of getting any dabs off it, or anything else. All lost by pushing it into the soil and us pulling it out again.'

Jack had a good look at the Witch's Tree. If anything, the front exposed roots were taller, creepier, the rain washing even more earth off. The chamber under them held a puddle, a lake, where ten years ago he and Mia might have put a paper boat. Quite a big tree, a metre across maybe. He stretched the trunk with his arms. The story was, the tree wandered about the Flats at night. With those roots, almost like the legs of a giant spider, you could imagine it lumbering around.

'I don't want to stick around, Jack. I've been here a few times, and there's nothing new for me beyond the knife.'

Jack sucked his lower lip thoughtfully. 'I'd like to time how long it takes to get from here to the snack place.'

He indicated his watch.

'Mine's better,' said Fayyad. 'It has a stopwatch feature.'

He took it off and handed it to Jack.

'Just press that button to start it and the same one to stop it.'

Jack started the watch and set off at run, well a sort of run, but it was too slippery to get up much speed. He kept a jog going, heading for the junction, nearly coming a cropper at one puddle. If he'd just done a murder, with the ground drier, he'd be going faster than this, but he wasn't about to break his neck.

At the junction, Jack began to walk, as from here, he would have been seen by the group having their snack.

He stopped the watch. Two minutes seven seconds.

Jack returned to the others, and showed them the time.

'I could've taken 20 seconds or more off in the weather we had on Saturday,' he said. 'Say one minute forty.'

'We have been working on two minutes,' said Fayyad. 'So give or take, much the same.'

They headed back, leaving the two CSIs at their final clear up. Twenty minutes later, Fayyad dropped him off at the shop, with ten minutes of those spent scrambling back down the path.

PART FOUR:
FINAL CIRCLE

Chapter 37

Back at the shop, he didn't get back to work, but sat in the office pondering what he'd seen. He had made tea, always a good catalyst for thought. The knife, where it had been buried, the tree, the time to get from it to the snack area, the walkers' tales of where they had been.

It was coming together.

He phoned Deneb, managing to catch him in his office at the college, putting it on speakerphone so Mia could hear.

'I want to set up a meeting tonight,' he said. 'Can we have it at your place, at 8pm?'

'What for, Jack?'

'To fill you and everyone else in on the investigation. Good news for you, I think. So is your place OK?'

'How many people?'

Jack calculated. 'Eight.'

'I'll have to borrow chairs from downstairs. If you bring cups and plates. But yes, I can do it. I need some good news, so depressing this investigation. I am not sleeping well, worrying they'll find me out. I'll get a cake, some biscuits. Do you think coffee or tea is best?'

'Both,' said Mia.

'It will be done. I look forward to you coming.'

They ended the call.

'The big reveal,' exclaimed Mia, clapping her hands with glee.

'I'm hoping to catch one or two of them out. Now, we have to phone all the walkers. Get them there. We tell them, that everyone else has agreed to come.'

'I'm getting used to telling lies for you.'

'This is for the agency,' he said, a little peeved.

They divvied up who was to phone who.

'You phone Penny,' he said.

'With pleasure,' said Mia. 'She more than owes me a favour.'

They got to it. Out of earshot of each other, with Jack phoning from the shop.

Liz was easy, his coffee date with her paying off. Nova, no problem. With Phil, he said he would take him for a drink afterwards. The tricky one was Fiona. Jack did her last, so he could say truthfully, everyone else is coming.

'This is not you lying, is it, Jack?'

He said, 'Penny, Nova, Phil, Deneb and Liz will be there. Ask them if you like. Me too, of course. And I'll bring everyone up to date on the investigation.'

'I'm going out this evening,' she said.

'It's not compulsory, but the others will be there, and you will find out exactly where things are at.'

'I don't like this last-minute stuff.'

'Everyone else will be there.'

'How many more times are you going to say that?'

As many as I need to, he thought.

'Are you coming?' he said.

A long pause. One can but try, he thought, with no powers of arrest. Poirot always managed to get all the suspects in the lounge. Miss Marple too. He'd seen them on TV. All the suspects present. Not so easy with busy, suspicious people. You only need one crying off, and you've lost the completeness.

'I'll be there,' said Fiona. 'With great reluctance. It had better be worth it.'

She ended the call.

Jack sighed with relief. He went in to see Mia.

'How was Penny?'

'She was oh so sorry about causing me distress last night.' She threw her arms wide. 'Now come on, that's a much bigger lie than I was spinning her.'

Which one, thought Jack. He was teaching his daughter bad habits. Alison would go bananas.

'But she's coming,' said Mia.

They punched fists.

It was four o'clock. Jack got back to work. With most of the afternoon spent on detective stuff, he had to have something for the moose in the morning. He spent a while attaching the sides and tops to the counters. And then having got so far, he wanted to have them both finished.

Just after six, they were done. They locked up and headed home.

Chapter 38

It had been a feat of last-minute organisation, getting all and sundry to Deneb's flat. Describing the event either as a social or the latest news on the investigation, depending on whom Jack or Mia were talking to. Following up by text, giving time and place. Deneb had borrowed extra chairs from his downstairs neighbour. Jack was all for getting paper plates and cups, but Mia wouldn't have it. It all goes into landfill, she protested.

So Jack and Mia brought over every cup and plate he had, adding to Deneb's few. Mia made a cake, Deneb bought biscuits and more cake.

Coats were bundled onto his bed.

To begin with, the group milled, a social, chatting about the sudden storm, the deluge they had had that afternoon, where they were when the heavens opened. The lightning strikes, the thunder, and the amazing rainbow. Next week, the clocks go back, the calendar of walks, the New Year Trip to Scarborough. And the odd comment about what they were going to learn today.

Jack was looking at his watch every few minutes, as he ate too much cake.

Where was he?

At least, all the suspects were here. Liz in a long flowery dress, Penny in blue jeans and a floppy red top, Fiona in striking Afro-colours, red, yellow and blue. Phil wore a grubby t-shirt saying Black Sabbath, stained jeans and his walking boots. Nova in her navy dress suit she wore for work, having come straight over. Deneb too wore a suit, being the host; he had asked Jack several times, what was the right thing to wear?

What you feel comfortable in, Jack had told him. That is no help, Deneb protested. 'Is a suit OK?' Jack said it was rather formal, but it was alright.

DI Fayyad Kamani arrived. And Jack sighed with relief. His coat was taken, he carried a fabric bag, which he wouldn't let anyone handle. Kamani too wore a suit, making Deneb feel better. It must be OK, if a senior policeman was so attired.

Fayyad was given a coffee and shown a choice of cakes, opting for a slice of creamy coffee cake.

Jack said, 'Have you confirmation on Taplow?'

'He was at an auction in Hampstead. Lots of witnesses.'

Jack nodded. 'Had to be sure.' He clapped his hands and addressed the room. 'If you'd all be so kind as to sit down, we can fill you in on progress of the investigation.'

There was a shuffle for seats. Three squeezed on the sofa. Nova and Kamani took chairs. Jack stood, Mia sat on the floor. She was offered Deneb's chair but she declined.

Jack said, 'Thank you all for coming at such short notice. But we did want everyone here, as I am sure you all want to know where we are, and to be freed of suspicion. Most of you have met Detective Inspector Fayyad Kamani.'

'Good evening, everyone,' said Fayyad, smiling benignly.

There were puzzled nods all round, as they hadn't been told that he was coming.

'Why is another cop here?' said Fiona. 'One is one more than we need.'

'He has things to tell us,' said Jack.

'And the kid,' she said, indicating Mia. 'What is she doing here?'

'I am part of the investigating team,' said Mia.

Fiona laughed. 'Go investigate your homework, kid.'

'I am not at school,' she said. 'And I'd listen if I were you. You might learn something.'

'You gonna teach me, girl?'

'Just listen, that's all I'm saying. You want to know what we found out, listen. Don't have a go at me.'

'You are one cheeky child.'

'Thank you. You've got some cheek too.'

'Can we come to order,' said Jack.

'I was just sitting here quietly,' said Mia, 'when she started on me.'

'I have no idea why you are here,' said Fiona.

'Here she goes again. Just listen, madam, and you'll find out. OK. Now lay off me.'

'Please, both of you,' said Jack. 'We'll get nowhere with this sniping. Let's have some hush. And I'll put you in the picture.'

He waited. He could see Mia was still bruised, and knew Fiona liked the last word. She was sullen, but silent.

'So let's get going,' said Jack, hoping for no more interruptions. 'The first problem with a murder like this in a public place, is whether it was done by one of the group, or by someone not with the group. Let's look wider, at least to start with. Fayyad, can you fill us in on Mike Rayner? He was being investigated, I hear.'

Fayyad nodded. 'We had been keeping a close eye on Mike Rayner. He was within a few days of arrest. In short, he was a ruthless art dealer who bought and sold stolen paintings as well as having a more legitimate job as a hedge fund manager. He would have had enemies from his art dealings for certain. He cheated and connived, so we didn't rule out someone from these dealings being the killer.'

'Thank you, Fayyad.' Jack looked about the group, checking he had their attention. 'Mike was stabbed,' he went on. 'If he was killed by someone in the group, they would have had to get rid of the knife somewhere nearby. All of us had our backpacks searched as soon as the police arrived. No weapon was found. But someone not in the group would, I am sure, have taken the knife well away from the crime scene. There's a big lake a mile away on Leytonstone Flats, or he'd have gone even deeper into Epping Forest to dump it.

'I asked myself, what would I do with a knife if I had to dispose of one quickly near the Witch's Tree? The ground was soft with all the recent rain. So I'd go off the trail into the forest, not far, there's no time as I'd need to get back to the group. And I'd stick the knife in the ground, a few inches down, and cover it up with leaves.'

Jack turned to Fayyad. 'Can you tell us about finding the knife, Fayyad?'

'Sure. After chatting with Jack,' said Fayyad, 'the CSI team went over the area with a metal detector. And we found this,' he brought out a photo from his bag, 'a large kitchen-type knife, found about 10 yards into the wooded area, near the body.' He showed the photo around the circle. 'The condition of the knife shows that it hadn't been in the ground long. It has been sharpened. And forensics say it is most likely the weapon used.'

'Thank you,' said Jack. 'So the knife was disposed of close by, which means, most likely, one of us is the killer. There were seven of us on the walk apart from Mike. Let's consider who had a motive for murder.

'I shall begin with our host, Deneb.'

Deneb looked sheepish, wondering what Jack was about to reveal.

'Mike didn't like you. You had two sins in his eyes. You are Syrian and you crossed the Channel in a small boat with a people smuggler. Mike would have booted you out of the club if he could. He hated your sort. But hate generates hate, Deneb.'

'I didn't like him,' said Deneb. 'But I did not kill him.'

Jack turned from him.

'Liz.'

She sat up straight, tried to smile but failed.

'Your daughter Gill was assaulted by Mike. I'll not go into detail.' He couldn't. What he said was as much as he knew. 'She lives in Spain and recently was arrested for shoplifting. The judge has asked for a psychiatric report. You are sure there is a connection with the assault.'

'Of course there is,' snapped Liz. 'She was fine before she met that love rat.'

'We certainly know Mike was not a nice man, which is why there were so few on the walk. His philandering and showing off, put people off. But you all came. I would say, you all had a reason for being there, beyond walking.' He turned. 'Penny.'

She looked at him fiercely, as if daring him.

'You went out with Mike for a few weeks. And he raped you.'

There was an intake of breath around the room. Penny said nothing. Another dive into the unknown. More than a guess, considerably less than a certainty. But no denial.

'You, Phil. Mike bought a picture from you. Paid you a thousand pounds for it.'

'Well over the odds,' Phil told the room, beaming. 'He could've had it for two fifty.'

'But that was all he bought,' said Jack. 'One picture. You have tried ever since to sell him more, sending him photos of your latest, collaring him on walks, but he wouldn't bite.'

'All his dirty money,' exclaimed Phil. 'Ten thou on a watch, can you believe it, but anything else and he was as tight as a Whitstable oyster!'

'Resentment is a powerful motive,' said Jack. 'Fiona.'

'This is petty, amateur sleuthing,' she said. 'It's laughable.'

Jack ignored the brickbats.

'Your partner is an art dealer, Fiona. Penny's ex, George Taplow. Now there's a coincidence, if there's ever such a thing in a murder case. You got out of your depth, with investments among the big money players, but Mike cheated you. And you had to sell your flat. You are now living with Taplow. With no love for Mike Rayner.'

Fiona pursed her mouth as if to spit, but desisted.

'Nova,' said Jack. 'You claimed to be working for the Council, but you were, in fact, an undercover cop.'

'Investigating Mike Rayner's dealings in stolen art.'

'And going out with him,' sneered Penny. 'Sleeping with him. Her evidence is useless.'

'She has been stood down from the case,' said DI Kamani. 'As she is too involved.'

'I never slept with Mike,' said Nova. 'I went out with him, for sure. But I had my limits.'

'Mike Rayner didn't,' exclaimed Penny. 'He took what wasn't offered.'

Nova stiffened, but saw there was little sense arguing, as Penny had decided and would not budge.

'He showed you his art, Nova, boasted of it,' said Jack. 'You went to his flat any number of times. Cops don't get overpaid. A couple of those paintings and you'd be set up for life. Were you tempted?'

She half smiled, which suggested to him that she had, at the very least, thought about it.

'No.' The smile wiped away, clearly uncomfortable in front of her boss.

Not a motive you could half deny.

He let the various motives settle, with each of the walkers wondering about the others.

'So let's go to the time and place of the murder,' he began again. 'Mike was murdered at the Witch's Tree. And the group was on a snack break.'

'You have missed yourself out,' snapped Fiona. 'Tell us your motive.'

'I was invited on the walk by Penny,' said Jack. 'I had never seen Mike before.'

'So you say,' said Phil. 'For all we know, you could be a hit man.'

'Let's say I could be,' said Jack, and might have added that any of them could be. 'Let's consider what we were all doing at the time of the murder. The snack break. Compulsory, while Mike went to hunt for the Witch's Tree. You, Phil, went off a number of times.'

'Call of nature, man. For heaven's sake. So I drink a bit. It's no crime. But what goes in has to come out.'

'Including your resentment.'

Phil shrugged. A sort of 'no comment'.

Jack turned to Liz. 'You had resentment too, Liz. And you went off for quite a while.'

'I found a patch of *Amanita muscaria*. Common name, fly agaric, the spotty red mushrooms that gnomes sit on. I took photos.' She flashed her phone. 'No gnomes, I'm afraid. You can see the photos, if you want.'

'Your daughter in Spain is yet to be tried. Expenses racking up...'

'I came on the walk to make Mike pay. I admit it. How would it help, killing the rat!'

'Hatred is a prime motive.'

He turned to Deneb. 'You hated him too.'

'He was just another racist. I can't possibly kill them all.'

'You sat on your own, reading a scientific paper, or so you said. But who would notice if you disappeared for a few minutes?'

Deneb didn't reply.

'We come to Fiona and Penny, talking together during the snack break, so you say.'

'We do say that,' said Fiona. 'Penny was with me, until she went to talk to you.'

'And then you played the penny whistle. Do you recall what you played?'

'*When The Saints Come Marching In.*'

'Not quite apt for Mike Rayner. The Saints were definitely not marching in when he was stabbed.' He screwed his eyes and peered at her. 'It has bothered me. Why were you playing the penny whistle at all?'

'I am learning to play it,' she said. 'Therapy, you might say, reduces tension. It has been a fraught few months. The penny whistle is a tiny instrument, no weight, fits easily into a backpack.'

Jack nodded, and went on. 'You, Penny. You went over to talk to the man fiddling with the yogurt pot lid.'

'I had invited you on the walk,' she said. 'You looked lost, in need of company.'

'Thoughtful of you, Penny.'

Jack looked around the circle, the group waiting on him.

'This was an odd walk,' he went on. 'We all had our motives to kill Mike. I include myself as a potential hit man, to join you as a suspect.' He sucked his lower lip. 'He was killed at the Witch's Tree. As if that had been picked as the location. But that hardly makes sense. The killer couldn't have known in advance that Mike couldn't find it. Or that he would be there alone.'

'So we are all off the hook,' said Liz.

'Some of you are, some of you aren't,' he said. 'Of course, the killer couldn't know in advance, that Mike couldn't find the Witch's Tree, but once that occurred, the killer grabbed the opportunity. The walk had been on the website for three weeks. You knew the route, he had listed the stopping points. You planned to kill him somewhere on the walk, not sure where you would do it, so you pre-walked it, to find a good spot. But early on, Mike went off on his own. That was too good an opportunity to miss.'

They were all watching Jack, caught up in their own thoughts of innocence or guilt. Or of being wrongly accused by this upstart.

'The killer decided it was on.' He raised his hands, waved them to correct himself. 'Sorry, I meant to say killers. Two of you were in cahoots. One of you went straight to the Witch's Tree, the other went to find Mike. You phoned him, found him wandering, and you got him to accompany you to the Witch's Tree. I suspect he was annoyed at having to be helped, but not for very long, as at the tree, one of you stabbed him. The deed done, you had to dispose of the knife. Time was passing, you mustn't be missed. To the verge of the woods you went, stabbed the knife into the soft earth, covered the site with leaves, and quickly got back to the unsuspecting group. Once there, you had to be noticed.

So one played the penny whistle, and the other joined the man making a spoon for his yogurt...'

He stopped. It was out in the open.

'You stupid bitch!' exclaimed Fiona, 'inviting that over-smart sleuth.'

'Shut your penny whistling gob,' seethed her partner. 'How unbelievably stupid. Suddenly, for no reason, she takes out a whistle and serenades the group.'

Fiona jumped up, crossed the circle and slapped Penny round the face.

Penny's head flew to the side.

'She killed him,' she screamed. 'It was Fiona! She killed Mike!'

'Liar!' roared Fiona.

Kamani rose. He was in full DI mode.

He said, 'I am arresting you, Penny Hicks, and you, Fiona Jones, for the murder of Mike Rayner. You do not have to say anything. But it may harm your defence if you do not mention when questioned something which you later rely on in court. Anything you do say may be given in evidence against you.'

He took out two pairs of handcuffs from his bag and threw one pair to Nova.

'Cuff them.'

Chapter 39

The next morning, Mia again went to the shop early, Jack more leisurely. He'd had too much cake last night and was feeling somewhat bloated. He managed a bowl of muesli, but that was all he could take.

Last night, the others had stayed on a while after Penny and Fiona were taken away by the law. Reduced by three, remaining were: Jack, Deneb, Liz, Phil, Mia and Nova. All relieved to have the shadow of suspicion taken off them. Nova had been an arresting officer, and with Fayyad, she had taken the pair down to the awaiting police cars. Penny was put in the first car, with a uniformed driver and an officer. Fiona was put in the second, with Fayyad and a driver. Nova was ushered away, with her part as undercover cop, she must play no further part. She returned to Deneb's flat to join the group.

There had been only one topic of conversation. But shock and awe added spice to it, with a measure of relief that it wasn't them under arrest. Jack was unsure what to charge Deneb, and would have settled for £300. Mia said, No. You pay for skill, £750. She put it to Deneb, and he accepted, thanking Jack for doing an excellent job.

Jack came into the shop. The walk from home had settled his stomach somewhat. Heavy metal music was issuing from the office, along with a smell of hot fat and vinegar. Mrs Elks was there, her face contorted, no doubt, by the smell and the racket. She closed the office door, the music subdued but still too loud, and the smell hung around.

She wore a long dress with black and white vertical stripes, the jacket matching. It practically gave Jack vertigo. Mia later called it a zebra dress, then retracted the remark as unfair to zebras.

Mrs Elks flapped her hands as if deterring flies. 'The noise and smell is impossible. It stinks like a chip shop. The music isn't music, just a loud cacophony. In the shop, we will have gentle sounds, classical music, pacifying, not this angry music.'

You can play what music you like, he thought, when I'm gone. This is simply to annoy you.

'The smell will stick around for weeks.' She shook her head vigorously. 'Surely you don't eat such rubbish?'

'My daughter does,' he said. For once, he could truly lay it on his offspring. She had bought the 'rubbish'. He reckoned it was chips, utterly laced with vinegar. The fast food joints on the high street got going early to fatten up the schoolkids and workers prone to high cholesterol.

'You cannot have the office, not if you are going to stink it out and the shop too. No, no. I can't dictate your music choices, but have you no taste?'

He didn't like it much either, but would not admit it to the moose.

'We have a deal,' he said. 'For 50% off, I get the office for a year, rent free.'

'Impossible.' She threw her arms in the air to emphasise how impossible, the stripes running to her wrists. 'No office, and 80%,' she said. 'My final offer.'

The office door opened. The heavy metal twanged into the shop, rocking the windows and floor, as Mia came out.

'Do you want a chip, Dad, Mrs Elks?'

She had a box of chips practically floating in vinegar.

Mrs Elks grabbed the box of chips and flounced out the back. Presumably to the bin.

'She hates you,' said Jack.

'Isn't that what we want?'

Mrs Elks came back chipless. She slammed the office door.

'No cooked food, no political banners or anything like, and no horrible loud music, and I agree to 90%. My final, final offer.'

Part of Jack wanted to hold out, but he had no wish to have an office here. 80% had been breakeven, so 90% was OK. If there were no problems.

'Agreed,' he said.

They shook hands.

Mia frowned. She would have held out for the lot.

Mrs Elks took some papers out of her bag. Still holding two, two others fell to the ground. He noted they were contracts, one headlined 75%, the other 80%. He handed them to her. But she had two in her hand. One would be for 90%, the other, he would bet, for the full 100%.

He could change his mind, he'd signed nothing.

But they had shaken on it.

'I want to add the words,' she said, 'no cooked food, political material or loud music.'

'And I wish to add, that we can use the office until the work is completed.'

'We have a completion date,' she said severely. 'With penalties for late delivery. In the contract.'

'We do.'

'I agree. You may use the office. Keep it clean. No filthy chips, young lady.'

They handwrote the additions on the contract, signed them, and at the bottom signed again.

She left.

Mia watched her down the road, and then brought out from the office an air freshener. Jack hardly knew which smell was worse, vinegar-soaked chips or the aerosol spray.

Chapter 40

Nova called at his house on Saturday morning. While they were having tea, she took a pair of boots out of her backpack. Almost new, brown leather.

'Try them on,' she said.

As he did so, he said, 'Whose are they?'

'Guess.'

'They are expensive, hardly worn...'

'I couldn't get you one of his watches,' she said. 'This was the best I could do.'

'Isn't it against the law?'

She shrugged. 'He had four pairs of boots. One he was wearing on the walk, and he had two pairs at his flat, and a pair left at my flat.'

Jack knew that the number of pairs didn't make it more legal, just less likely anyone would notice a pair not there. But no name had been mentioned. So just a present from a girlfriend. And he'd not ask her how the boots got left at her flat.

He walked about his sitting room in them.

'Some boots,' he said, kneeling down, feeling the vibrant leather. 'Superb. I wonder how much they cost him.'

She shrugged. 'Don't wear them for work.'

Half an hour later, they strolled up the road, Nova in her green anorak, yellow woolly hat, red trousers and expensive walking boots. Jack in his new boots, blue jeans, black hoody and black woolly hat. He favoured black as it didn't show the dirt. Both had backpacks.

The sun was shining on the last day before the clocks went back. Tomorrow they would be on winter time, or

Greenwich Mean Time as Jack knew full well, as it was Universal Time that astronomers kept to.

A clear blue sky above, if it stayed meant a good night for star watching, but today's walk would be enough outdoor time. Mia was with her mother. To come to some sort of arrangement, Alison had said. About schooling, and where she would live.

For a socialist, it struck him that Mia was quite a negotiator. She had got £750 from Deneb, not that he'd griped, happy enough that he wouldn't get a thorough going over by the cops. She would have held the moose to the original price, had it been down to her.

So would she go back to school? And live with her mother as well as him. Her choice utterly. But she couldn't work for *Forest Gate Investigations*, as he couldn't see it working for him either. His living was as a builder, who might do some sleuthing if a client ever turned up.

They dropped into the Co-op. Today, Jack had brought a spoon, a knife too. He figured a spoon could double as a fork. They bought various snack items: bananas, yogurts, nuts and raisins, and crisps. Mia insisted that he should not buy bottled water. It was an utterly shameful capitalist trick, and cost a thousand times more than that coming out of the tap. She had given him a bamboo water bottle. Nova had a steel one, courtesy of the cops, who had fully kitted her out for her undercover role.

When they got to the Flats, Nova put on her gaiters, black plastic fabric that fitted round her lower ankles and lower legs.

'Keeps mud off your trousers,' she said.

She advised him to do what the old-timers do and stick his trousers in his socks. It would work to some extent. He considered it, then did so. Might as well keep some mud off.

They crossed the Flats, and discussed how they might stop arguing in the future. Nova was the navigator, using an app on her phone that had the trails through the forest. She had a backup power pack in case her phone battery died.

'You could agree with me,' she said.

'Or vice versa,' said Jack.

Neither workable solutions.

The rest of the week had been rain free, so the Flats had dried out to some extent, more like last Saturday than the storm-soaked ground that Jack and Fayyad had experienced.

She said, 'You were fond of Penny.'

'I didn't know her.' He shrugged. 'We only had one date really. Got on, she's attractive, but it wouldn't have lasted.' He laughed. 'Can you imagine me with a professor?'

She could, but didn't answer the question.

'Penny has thrown everything away, her career,' she said, 'her good name, her freedom. If only she'd never met Mike Rayner.'

'He didn't do anyone any good, not even himself.'

And then he thought of the boots he was wearing, but they hadn't been granted by Mike. Jack would not ask how they were obtained, but oh, they were some boots. He must get some brown polish, keep them pukka. Though he knew he probably wouldn't.

After an hour or so, they came to the Witch's Tree. A couple of small children were crawling about the chamber beneath the exposed roots.

'One of the killers was presumably behind the tree in wait, while the other brought him in,' she said. 'Do we know who did the stabbing?'

'I certainly don't.' He shrugged. 'They'll blame each other. So only they will know.'

'Most likely they'll both go down for it,' she said. 'Joint enterprise, they call it.'

'We could ask the tree who did the stabbing,' he said.

'I don't speak tree-ish.'

They walked on, a few hundred yards to Bush Road, much drier than with Fayyad trying his hardest to keep shoes and trousers from getting splattered, and headed to the Green Man roundabout, then over to Leytonstone Flats.

It was companionable. And it struck Jack that maybe walks with Nova might work, now he had these amazing boots. Out in the wild, she couldn't just race off when the call came for the next murder investigation.

By the lake at Highams Park, they had their snack, watching the ducks and geese, enjoying the autumn colour.

'Will you come to Tate Britain with me?' she said.

He thought on this horror, an art gallery, he had tried them with Alison.

'If you promise not to abandon me there.'

They were quiet a while, a soft breeze rippling the surface of the lake. Two swans, so regal and utterly white drifted by, and a couple of coots with their white hats.

She said, 'There were two of us arriving at almost the same time, that night on the Flats. Did you mean to continue that way?'

Jack was eating a yogurt, with a proper spoon.

He said, 'I didn't know where I was with either of you.'

'She came dressed to kill.'

'I think to get information out of me.'

'Could you have held out?' she said with a wry smile.

'I went with you over the Flats, remember.'

'I do.' She kissed him on the cheek. 'It was a beautiful evening, cloudy but wonderful company.'

'Pity how it ended.'

They embraced, cheek against cheek, hands clutching hands. And then, for a little time, seeing the light caught in their eyes, the sun and rippling water, words dissolved in warmth and need.

They continued the walk, through the leaf-covered trails, autumn colour in the remnant of leaves on the beech, oaks and hornbeams. The sun shining, mottling the path, mushrooms on the ground, on rotting stumps, and on the side of living trees. Nova had the phone in one hand, to navigate, and the other hand in his.

Thank you!

I am grateful to every reader who finishes one of my novels. I have taken you on a journey which I hope you have enjoyed. There are plenty of things you could have been doing, other than reading this book. So, thank you for your time. If you liked *Jack Takes A Walk*, here's what you can do next:

I'd appreciate a review. In that way, you can help me tell other readers about my books. Without reviews authors get few sales. So I'd be grateful for your review to help this series get on the move.

You can get a FREE ebook of *Murder at Any Price* if you sign up for my readers' list.

You may give it to a friend if you wish. When you sign up for my readers' list you will receive my regular newsletter. This will give you news about me, what I'm reading, and tell you about my future books, PLUS a variety of giveaways.

Sign up at my website:
DerekSmithWriter.com

Books by DH Smith

Jack Bell

These are all standalone novels and can be read in any order. They are:

- *Jack of All Trades*
- *Jack of Spades*
- *Jack o'Lantern*
- *Jack By The Hedge*
- *Jack In The Box*
- *Jack On The Tower*
- *Jack Recalled*
- *Jack At Death's Door*
- *Jack At The Gate*
- *Jack In The Dust*
- *Jack At The Lodge*
- *Jack In The Garden*
- *Jack Fell Down*
- *Jack In Clink*
- *Jack Takes A Walk*

Other Books

Writing A Crime Novel

Books by Derek Smith

All my books, other than the *Jack of All Trades* series and *Murder at Any Price*, are written under the name Derek Smith.

Fantasy
Hell's Chimney
The Prince's Shadow

Other Books
Strikers of Hanbury Street (short stories)
Catching Up (poetry)

Young Adult Novels
Hard Cash
Half a Bike
Fast Food
Frances Fairweather Demon Striker!

Children's Novels
The Good Wolf
Feather Brains
Baker's Boy

For Younger Children
The Magical World of Lucy-Anne
Lucy-Anne's Changing Ways
Jack's Bus

About the Author

I live in Forest Gate in the East End of London. In my working life, I have been a plastics chemist, a gardener and a stage manager before becoming a professional writer. I began with plays, working with several theatre companies, and had a few plays on radio and TV, as well as on the stage.

In the early 80s I became involved in running a co-operative bookshop and vegetarian café in Stratford, where I learned to cook, and had my first go at writing a novel. The first was a mess, and, after too many rewrites, binned. The transition from drama to novels took me a couple of years to get to grips with.

My first success was a young adult novel, *Hard Cash*, published by Faber. Buoyed up by this, I stuck with children's work, did school visits, and made a hand to mouth living as a full time author, topped up with some evening class work in creative writing at City University and the Mary Ward Centre in Holborn. A few adult fiction titles appeared from time to time, between the children's list, and I have since been working more in that direction with my *Jack of All Trades* series.

DerekSmithWriter.com

The book you've been reading
was designed by Lia
at Free Your Words...

lia@freeyourwords.com